"Two thousand pounds might be cheap to you..."

Doro started to object, but Garreth cut her off.

"But it's wealth to Tom," he said. "That's why it's better that he lost a lot than just a little. I expect he's cured of gambling," he ended grimly.

"I suspect you're right. I have you to thank for easing my mind."

She smiled up at him. "I suppose you'll be glad when the season is over and we return to Marvale. We have certainly been a trial to you."

When he spoke, his voice was low and distant.

"Have you heard me complain, Doro?"

"You're far too much of a gentleman for that," she said.

"Will you always refuse to know me, Doro? Will you always refuse to see that I may have my own reasons?"

He bowed and turned back to pass through the gate and into his own garden, leaving her looking after him and wondering what he could possibly mean."

SWEET DORO

DIXIE LEE McKEONE

Harlequin Books

TORONTO • NEW YORK • LONDON
AMSTERDAM • PARIS • SYDNEY • HAMBURG
STOCKHOLM • ATHENS • TOKYO • MILAN

Published September 1989

ISBN 0-373-31109-5

CHAPTER ONE

MARVALE WAS SHOWING its age. The ancient pile that had sheltered the Lindsterhope family for three centuries towered in its neglect, all the more noticeable because of its size and past glories. The lawn, which had once been a weedless expanse of green, was kept short by a small flock of sheep, which muddied the banks of the ornamental lake as they stood to drink.

The hedges and walks of the formal gardens now knew the touch of only one aging gardener, who occasionally found time to trim the nearest hedges when he was not busy with the vegetables. He lacked the strength to cut and pull away the ivy that crept up the walls of the manor house, or to chop the dead limbs from the ancient oaks.

But the damage caused by neglect was superficial. The old stone walls were sturdy, and no dry rot had reached the timbers supporting the floors and attics. The slate roof which had been repaired twenty years before still kept out the storms of the Yorkshire winter and the rains of its summer.

In the long drawing room, Lady Dorothea Sailings, the dowager Baroness of Lindsterhope, Doro to close friends and family, lifted a large, ornate silver pot and poured tea into chipped cups. She no longer worried about the inadequate china, the faded drap-

eries, which showed numerous careful mends, nor the
worn cushions on the confidante and chairs. She had
lived with them too long to let them seriously disturb
her, especially since they would soon be replaced.

The five people taking tea in the drawing room were
aware that a lack of capital to restore Marvale was not
the problem. The Lindsterhope fortune was large and
had been growing for years. Its inaccessibility was the
difficulty, but in a few months that, too, would be a
thing of the past. Tom Sailings, the young twelfth
Baron of Lindsterhope, would soon reach his majority, and it was then that an onerous and stringent trust
would be brought to an end. As the time grew shorter
both the family and the servants of Marvale looked
toward to the future with increased hope.

Dorothea's chief concern that bright afternoon was
the interest their two guests displayed in the time when
Tom came into his inheritance. Their delight and the
plans for the distribution of that hoarded wealth
seemed to weigh far more heavily on their minds than
it did on the Sailings'.

The owner and lord of the well-known manor house
was at that moment gingerly testing a chair. Satisfied
that it was sturdy, he picked it up and moved it to
within easy conversational distance of his sister, Farrie, and their female guest, Elsa, seated on a confidante. Tom, at twenty, was less mature in manner than
most young men who had been through the polishing
of a good school. He was of barely medium height,
with light brown hair and dark eyes accentuating the
vivid complexion of a youth who preferred outdoor
activities. As he arranged the chair to his satisfaction,
he moved with the impetuousness of a boy trying to

emulate a companion whose poise and style left him considerably in awe.

"Seems safe enough, though I'd be careful how I sat, Sir Gerald." He laughed with false bravado, to cover his embarrassment over the condition of his home.

"It can't be as bad as that," the ex-cavalry officer replied as he put one hand on the back of the chair and shook it, making his own test for stability. Dorothea could not but notice that he had used the excuse of shaking the chair to turn it slightly. When he sat, his back was to the tea table, effectively shutting her out of the circle of conversation.

She was not surprised. His veneer of good manners was parchment thin and he lacked subtlety. For that she was grateful; had he been a true gentleman, she was not at all sure she would have seen his motives so clearly. No more experienced than her charges in the matter of adventurers, she might have been as taken in as Tom.

But fortunately, he had showed his true nature at their first meeting. As a visitor to the area, and therefore not privy to the local gossip, he had taken in the threadbare clothing of the Sailings and made it plain that he had no time for shabby gentility.

When he learned his error and immediately changed his attitude, Dorothea had his measure. Try as she would, her innate good manners could not disguise her suspicion of him, and he read it in her eyes. Like many who care nothing for the feelings of others, he was nevertheless sensitive to opinions of those who might have an effect on his comfort. Recognizing her wariness, he showed a marked resentment of her.

As soon as he came into possession of the knowledge that the straightened finances of the Sailings would soon take a sudden and fortunate turn, he made Farrie the object of his gallantry. His suit was doomed to failure. The shy young lady withdrew into an uncomfortable silence in his presence. His extravagant compliments only caused her to blush, grow nervous and find any excuse to absent herself when he came to call.

Dorothea wondered if Farrie's disinclination for his company was due to her shyness. She held the private opinion that the girl might be a shrewder judge of character than her years and experience could explain.

Not a man to see a failure as his own doing, and having recognized that Dorothea did not trust him, he appeared to blame Dorothea for this lack of success.

But while Farrie avoided him and Dorothea worried, Tom had found a friend. He saw nothing amiss with the gallant ex-officer, and was delighted with his company, so Sir Gerald had no reason to give up his hopes of getting his hands on a part of the Sailings fortune.

Tom would be the one who would control the bulk of the estate, and Sir Gerald had another way of attaching himself to a full purse. He had leased a small house on the other side of the village and had brought his sister Elsa to stay with him. He clearly hoped she would snare the unworldly Tom.

The pair had made it a practice to drop in at teatime several times a week, and while Dorothea and Farrie deplored the habit, Tom was always glad to see Sir Gerald, though he did not seem to give Elsa a thought, apparently considering her to be Farrie's friend.

So when Sir Gerald turned the chair to exclude Dorothea from the conversation, she was just as glad. If she were not caught up in the conversation, she would be free to listen, always on the alert for any danger to her charges.

"You think not?" Tom went on about the condition of the furniture, unaware of Sir Gerald's ploy. "Yesterday I was sent sprawling when a leg gave way on a stool—another piece consigned to the lumber room to await a good joiner. Have to hire a man full time, the way the place is coming to bits."

The last was said with a straightening of his shoulders and a perceptible lowering of vocal timbre, as if he were trying to fit himself to the responsibilities that would soon be his. He came to stand by the tea table, signifying his willingness to hand round the cups.

He took two, one for Farrie, and one for Elsa Palvley, who shared the confidante. As lord of the manor, he could reasonably have left the handing about to his sister or Doro, but the pride of his position had not entered his head.

To one who watched him with a loving eye, vulnerability seemed to be his major trait. Raised on the edge of penury, he never had occasion to develop the pride of fortune or position. It was therefore not surprising that he was more than casually gratified by the attention of a man with a reputation for dash and bravery.

She could not blame Tom for his attachment to the ex-officer. In the recent war on the Continent, he had been mentioned in the despatches and his name had often been used synonymously with daring exploits.

Sir Gerald comported himself with an elegance of style and poise that Dorothea felt to be subtly dandified, but to Tom and Farrie, who had never had the benefit of society, he seemed elegance itself.

As Tom handed the teacups to the young ladies on the sofa, it occurred to Dorothea that two young females of the same age could not have been more different.

Miss Frances Sailings, eighteen-year-old sister to the young baron, was like him with her light brown hair, dark eyes and a reserved nature. Her round gown, slightly outdated and overworn, bespoke a young woman of innocent nature. The intricate embroidery at the hem and the neck was due to her own labour and testified to a love of beauty. Her reservations about their visitors took the course of extreme shyness and she sat with her eyes upon the floor. Her fingers twisted a lace handkerchief as she warred with her shyness and the need to carry a part of the conversation for the sake of good manners.

In contrast, Miss Elsa Palvley was a titian-haired beauty whose clothing was in the latest fashion. While her riding dress was in design most unexceptionable, its close fit, the jauntiness of her hat and the way her curls trimmed her face showed she was a young woman who was well aware of her charms. Her manner of showing them off brought her to the brink of being considered fast.

In the month that Sir Gerald and Elsa had been staying in the neighbourhood, Dorothea had become unpleasantly aware that Elsa was giving her brother her wholehearted cooperation in trying to attach Tom's affections. Their lack of success had come about because, not being in the petticoat line, Tom had been oblivious to their attempts.

As Tom handed Elsa the tea, she smiled up at him with a sultriness that was out of place in a young woman of her age.

"My lord, I'd not be overly concerned with the furnishings, because it's only a matter of time until you will be consigning them all to the lumber room and ordering the best London has to offer...." She paused and made a pretty pout of vexation. "Gerald, you let me forget the publication, even though I warned you I especially wanted to bring it."

"So I did," Sir Gerald said promptly.

Dorothea wondered if the rapidity of his answer was due to a rehearsal, or if her suspicion of him was causing her to read a sinister meaning into the most casual of remarks.

"Elsa is consumed with ideas you might use here at Marvale," Sir Gerald said, leaning forward, as if imparting some guilty secret, though he gave his sister a teasing look. "She will not tell you so, but she ordered the catalogue especially for you."

"You mustn't say so, Gerald," Elsa chided. "I would be most put out if the baron thought our concern to be meddling in his affairs."

"Oh, not at all," Tom said over his shoulder as he returned to the tea table to procure a cup for his male guest.

"Though she is my sister, I will tell you you could do worse than to be guided by Elsa. She is most knowledgeable about what the current fashions are in town, and you'll not want to be behind hand, of course."

Dorothea glanced up to see a slight frown crease Tom's brow, and she ducked her head to hide the twitching of her lips. Sir Gerald did not understand Tom nor the life they had lived, nor the close relationship that existed between Tom, Farrie and Doro; and because he did not, he had erred.

Dorothea had been Farrie's age when her first season had been interrupted by her father's death. The financial difficulties faced by her family had caused her brother to accept the offer in her behalf from William Sailings, the elderly eleventh Baron of Lindsterhope. The inducement which had won her brother's approval of the marriage had been the generous settlements offered by the wealthy old gentleman. His need had not been for a wife, but for a surrogate mother to his orphaned grandchildren.

Dorothea had buried her own dreams when she came to live at Marvale, but William Sailings had been kind and considerate, and she had given her heart to two-year-old Farrie and four-year-old Tom. The first four months of her marriage had been pleasant and luxurious if not exciting. Then the elderly baron suffered a stroke that left him an invalid.

They feared for his life for several weeks, but he slowly gained the use of one hand and became able to speak again. That was when they learned the illness had brought on a reversal of personality. The kind and generous man that Dorothea had married became a suspicious, clutch-fisted tyrant. Those who continued to hold him in esteem explained to themselves and others that he was making a desperate, if misguided, attempt to protect the fortune of young Tom, his successor. Unfortunately, for the servants and the Sailings, he saw it as his duty to reduce the expenditures of the household and Dorothea's personal allowance to meagre proportions.

For ten years he ruled the household from his bed until he suffered his final and fatal stroke. That had been six years before, but the disorder of his mind that had caused their discomfort was still continuing.

His irrational fear that Dorothea might leave his grandchildren without a guidance had been responsible for his making a will leaving both her dower portion and his heir's inheritance in trust until Tom came of age. The trust had provided only the barest stipend for the upkeep of Marvale and the family. Even the administrators abhorred the unfairness of the arrangement, but though the aging William Sailings had suffered a change of personality, he had not lost one whit of his business accumen. They were unable to overset the will.

Dorothea, Tom and Farrie had been put to uncomfortable shifts to maintain themselves, and had derived their solace from planning for the time the trust ended. The knowledge had been their mainstay and the support for their spirits.

In suggesting that Elsa be Tom's guide in the refurbishing of Marvale, Sir Gerald was not only attempting to remove the young man from the influence of his sister and Dorothea, he was negating all those years of mutual support.

"Doubtless we will need some advice," Tom answered slowly, carefully choosing his words while he waited for Dorothea to fill his cup, "but you must know Farrie and Dorothea have made some plans.

Dorothea says there are many pieces of considerable value that should be preserved."

"Then perhaps she would like to take them to dower house and look after them herself," Sir Gerald answered, obviously nettled by what he considered the young man's defection from his influence.

Well, that was plain enough, Dorothea thought. In her more sympathetic moments she wondered if she were being fair to Sir Gerald, asking herself if she could be mentally maligning the man's character because of her concern for her charges. But if in his mind he was already consigning her to dower house, then he did plan on arranging a marriage between Tom and Elsa. If he could replace her influence with his and his sister's, Tom's fortune would not last long. A cold chill ran up her spine.

"Doro in dower house?" Farrie ejaculated, so stung by the idea she forgot her discomfort.

"I sh-shouldn't like that at all." Tom stuttered. His speech defect appeared only when he was too emotional to keep it under control. It warned those that knew him of just how deeply he disapproved of the suggestion. As if to reinforce his desire to keep Dorothea at Marvale, he dropped to the chair by the tea table, ignoring the one he had placed near the confidante.

Realizing the difficulty of carrying on a conversation when his host sat behind him, Sir Gerald rose and rotated the chair on one leg. The action gave him time to rethink his remarks, and when he sat down again, he gave Dorothea a smile she took to be condescending.

"My dear young man, you take too much for granted. Would you condemn her to remain here, when in her own household she would be free to make a new life? Lady Dorothea is a lovely woman and still young enough to marry again."

Clearly such a thought had never occurred to Tom, who turned to look at her with eyes bright with surprise and mischief.

"Should you like to marry again, Doro? Shall you go to London and parade around in society, setting all the men's hearts to fluttering?"

"In a lace cap and carrying my sewing basket?" Dorothea retorted, busying herself with rearranging the tea things to hide her unwillingness to take further part in the conversation.

In truth the suggestion had brought back memories and dreams she had thought buried beyond retrieval sixteen years before when she learned she was to marry the late Baron of Lindsterhope. She resolutely pushed them aside, concentrating on the conversation which flowed between Sir Gerald and Tom.

"And you will be bringing a new baroness into Marvale before long, unless I miss my guess," their guest was saying. His eyes strayed suggestively to his sister, but Tom's blank look showed he had not caught the obvious hint.

Dorothea felt the cold prickle of fear. Gossip suggested the ex-cavalry officer was living far beyond his means and was being hounded by creditors. When she was younger she had been a reader of the most time-wasting novels, and so every instance of devious trickery about which she'd read came to mind as she considered what means Sir Gerald could employ to trick Tom into marrying Elsa.

"In any event you must come over and let Elsa show you the newest styles from London," Sir Gerald went on. "I know she is so disappointed that she did not bring the papers with her. Are you free later this week?"

"I'll certainly try to come," Tom said readily. "It's jolly good of her to take the trouble," he added, "but I've promised Doro and Farrie to accompany them on a shopping trip to Scarborough." He turned to Dorothea. "Have you set the day you want to go?"

"I'm afraid not," Dorothea answered, keeping her voice even. "The weather seems to be changeable and Farrie has not been in the best of health lately. Could you send a note around to Sir Gerald when we can manage a visit without risk of her taking a chill?"

The steely glint in the gentleman's eye told her she had scored a hit by including herself and Farrie in the invitation. It also confirmed her opinion that he had hoped to have Tom visit alone. But that teasing remark of Tom's about London had given Dorothea an idea. She let the talk flow unheard as she formed a plan.

Twenty minutes later, Tom escorted their visitors to their carriage, a courtesy which would provide him an opportunity to see Sir Gerald's newly acquired team of high steppers.

In the drawing room, Farrie and Dorothea opened their sewing baskets to continue with their embroidery, when Farrie sighed.

"I shudder to think what will happen to Marvale if Miss Palvley has a hand in its refurbishing." Then realizing she had spoken with unbecoming criticism, she coloured slightly. "That was an unworthy remark, but I cannot help wishing the Palvleys would return to London."

"Or that we could?" Dorothea asked softly.

"Us?" Farrie was startled into a moment's silence. Then she nodded. "I have no desire to go among so many strangers, but if it would remove Tom from Sir Gerald's influence . . . Could we do it, Doro?"

Knowing she would have Farrie's support in her plan, Dorothea continued to develop the details while the younger lady left the room to search out a skein of robin's-egg blue with which to finish a length of embroidery. In her absence, Tom returned. He settled on the sofa she had just vacated, his face aglow with interest.

"Now, sweet Doro, what are you about?" he demanded. "And don't tell me nothing, because you are quite transparent. Your eyes suddenly sparkled when an idea occurred to you, and Farrie's health is perfect. Are you planning something scandalous?"

"Not quite scandalous," Dorothea said, smiling at him, and finding his levity contagious, she squirmed a little on her chair, excited by her daring, though she knew she must be cautious about how she presented her plan to Tom.

"When Sir Gerald spoke of the possibility of my marriage, he set me to thinking—"

"Oh-ho!" Tom's eyes lit up. "Is there a dashing beau in the background? Why have I not suspicioned it? Who is it? The vicar, the squire . . . ?"

"Don't be silly." Dorothea blushed, quite unable to hide the embarrassment of his acute observation, though he could not know her hopes of romance had died with her marriage sixteen years before.

"It was not myself I was thinking of, but Farrie. If you hold by your plan to increase her dowry, she will be in a dangerous position, being so innocent of society. There are so many fortune-hunters in town." She did not express her opinion that there was one in their own neighbourhood.

"Of course I'll increase it, just as soon as I'm able. There's no reason I should not. And you are correct—we'll have to protect her," Tom said. "She is quite the little goose, isn't she?"

Though Farrie was not the only one, Dorothea thought it best not to mention it.

"She is, and while we can try to protect her, we cannot shield her heart from the charm of fortune-hunters," Dorothea said. "It's been worrying me for some time."

A little crease developed between Tom's brows. "But what's to be done? In order to learn, she has to have exposure to them, doesn't she?"

Dorothea readily agreed. "But what if she could learn that lesson before she was vulnerable?"

"I don't understand."

Could she enlighten him, Dorothea wondered, when she was not clear on anything save her need to remove Tom and Farrie from the clutches of an unscrupulous man? Would the only explanation she could contrive deceive him about her real purpose? She knew he would not see Sir Gerald in the same light that she did.

"I'm thinking we should go to London now," she said in a rush, getting out the crux of her idea. "We must live in a moderately quiet state, but we will be there in time for the season, and since Farrie cannot be considered to have a large dowry at present, she will be in a position to see the poses of the matchmakers and fortune-hunters without being in danger of being caught up in their schemes.''

Tom stared at her wide eyed. ''I think the idea is grand, but how can we manage before my birthday?''

''You remember I have that small inheritance from Cousin Margaret....''

''But you were to hold that in reserve!''

''Why should we? My dower portion will also be released at your majority, and while Cousin Margaret's gift is not enough to go far, it will take us to town and buy us a few niceties. Remember, this is to save Farrie from heartbreak later.''

''I th-think it's a bang-up plan!'' Tom's excitement showed in his stutter as it finally dawned on him that they could really go. ''She'll be thrilled.'' He paused, a shy smile transforming his face from that of a young man into a shy boy. ''I wouldn't mind looking about a little myself. When would we go?''

''We can start our preparations today,'' Dorothea said as she stood up from the tea table. ''We must write to Mr. Haworth, telling him we will be opening Lindsterhope House, and we will take most of the servants from Marvale to prevent having to hire more. You will be quite busy giving instructions to the bailiff and seeing to the travel arrangements for the servants, I'm afraid. Shall you mind?''

''Not at all, but I must send a note round to Sir Gerald, to tell him we are going.''

''You can do that later,'' Dorothea said, hoping her effort to put off warning the ex-officer was not too blatant. "First we must start our preparations, and you know he will understand. He has himself suggested you need town bronzing, so he must approve of the scheme."

"Yes he w-will," Tom acquiesced, too excited to see through Dorothea's ploy. "Farrie will be in transports." He paused. "But we cannot tell her the real reason, of course."

"No, we cannot," Dorothea admitted, but Farrie would know the truth, though the young lady was wise enough to hide her distrust of Sir Gerald from her brother.

Once they were in town, clothing would be their first need if they were to go into society at all, Dorothea decided. She would write to her childhood friend, Sally, and ask for advice, though for the present she would not aspire to her friend's social circle. It would be ten months before they could afford to travel in Lady Jersey's set.

ELMRIDGE, THE ANCIENT HOME of the Marquess of Ridgeley, was not quite as large as Marvale, but it was as well kept as Marvale was seedy. Not one wayward tendril of an overgrown vine dared mar the perfection of the imposing edifice. Not one stone was out of place on the fences that encompassed the several tenant farms.

The easterly view of the small dining room at Elmridge gave the room a sunny aspect in the mornings. Its proportions were not handsome, but the appointments showed care and glistened in the sunlight coming through the sparkling clean panes of the partially opened French windows. The furnishings were not in the current mode, but they were sturdy and comfortable, exactly suiting the two people who currently partook of their breakfasts at one end of the heavily laden table.

The breakfast room, like every other chamber in Elmridge, showed the efforts of an energetic and dutiful housekeeper, but it was apparent at a glance that no mistress graced the principal seat of the Marquess of Ridgeley. The three chairs set along the inner wall of the room were at present holding such articles as the two men thought wise to have at hand. Two curly-brimmed beaver hats, two pairs of gloves and two driving coats, each with a modest three capes, lay on the needlepoint seat covers, along with several sporting and farming publications.

The dark, ruggedly handsome man who sat at the head of the table was Viscount Tolver, master of Elmridge by right and responsibility given him in the will of a man he never met. At thirty-five, lines of a strong-willed nature marked his face. He appeared to be a man more at ease in ordering a cavalry troop or mastering a sailing ship than in a drawing room.

To one unaccustomed to the details of a coat cut by Weston, he appeared to be tailored in exquisite fashion. Those who knew better would recognize in his Bath blue superfine coat the hand of a talented local tailor and the care of a first-class valet. He was dressed in top boots as benefitted a gentleman preparing for a journey, which the driving coat on the chair suggested. At the moment he was relaxing over a second cup of coffee, reading a letter from his solicitor.

To Lord Tolver's right sat his ward, who bore the title of Marquess of Ridgeley and was of far different appearance. His hair was too light to be considered gold, and soft waves framed his face, which had a fair, clear complexion and ruddy cheeks. The marquess had just entered his nineteenth year, but his enthusiasm and his alert, enquiring gaze made him appear younger. He glanced up from the letter he was perusing, his face lit with amusement.

"Amelia says bonnets called Villagers are all the crack in town. They make her look a quiz..." the marquess commented as he returned to the cross-written letter. A burst of laughter followed further perusal, after which the young man sobered. As he read his lips tightened perceptibly.

The viscount glanced up from his own letter and saw the frown on the younger man's face. He ruthlessly repressed his smile as he went back to his own correspondence.

"No! I'll not have that!" the marquess asserted as he read. "I'll tell her so soon enough!"

"Something amiss, Charlie?" the viscount asked as he put aside his letter and picked up another. He was never much put out by the tiffs between Lady Amelia Easterly and Lord Ridgeley, who had been raised on neighbouring properties and who had been best friends and foes since their nursery days.

"Garreth, she says I'm to lead her out at her ball. That's cheek, not even asking if I want to, and she ought to know I don't, taking the floor with every eye in the place on us," the young marquess said, still inspecting the letter as if he could find some denial of the unwelcome demand.

"Much choice you'll have, once Amelia makes up her mind." Lord Tolver chuckled, looking over a bill from a local merchant and wondering how one household contrived to use so many candles. "Besides," he continued, "I thought the main reason we were going was to be present at her come-out ball. And you'd better get yourself in hand. Once the young bucks in town see her, you'll be cut out if you don't shake yourself into doing the pretty."

Lord Tolver knew Charlie was not yet in the petticoat line, or he would never had spoken so casually. The marquess was to all practical purposes no more than a schoolboy, and far less mature than his female friend, who was a year younger.

"I wonder anyone should have her if she takes to such starts, telling a fellow what he's to do without considering how he feels about it," Charlie said, proving his guardian's opinion of him. "She'll look nohow if I just don't lead her out when the time comes."

The viscount was in the act of finishing his coffee when he paused, the cup chin high and forgotten. He stared at his ward.

"Charlie, you wouldn't do that!" Lord Tolver was too stunned to do more than voice those words.

"Someone's coming." Charlie flung down the letter and rose from his chair at the sound of horses and wheels coming at a fast clip up the drive. "Who could be visiting so early?" he said, striding toward the French windows.

"Damn visitors, let them come to the front door. Charlie, come back here. I want to talk to you."

Hearing the unusual severity in his guardian's voice, Charlie turned and started back toward the table. He took his seat again, his expression puzzled and concerned.

Garreth was just gathering his thoughts, but he was not given time to express them. The arriving vehicle had not passed on to the front door, but had come to a halt outside the dining room. Booted footsteps sounded on the flagstone terrace outside the windows. A strong young voice shouted for someone to hold the brutes.

Both the viscount and the marquess looked up as the French windows were flung open by an excited young gentleman who at first glance appeared to be of an age with the marquess.

"Charlie, come see what m'father brought back from Exeter!" Mr. George Finhurst was the son of the local squire and two years junior to Lord Ridgeley. One look at his round, freckled face showed something unusual had brought him out so early in the day. "Come and see! A phaeton and pair for my birthday! Morning, sir, trust I see you well," he added, belatedly remembering to extend his courtesy to the viscount.

The news of his friend's gift had driven the viscount's order from Charlie's mind. "Gammon! You'll be in a ditch before the day is out," the marquess said, rushing to the window and stepping out onto the terrace.

"Much you know!" his friend retorted, following him. "I may not be a whip in your class, but I can stick to my leaders."

"Lord, what a turnout! That teams looks high couraged."

"Afraid I might miss you," George said. "Wanted to show them to you before you left for London." He tugged at his gloves and looked up at the sky. "Doubt you'll have much time to think of horses in town, but when you come back, I'll be ready to give you a run for your guineas."

Lord Tolver didn't doubt George would try, and watching the boys through the open French doors, he gave a barely perceptible nod of approval at the squire's wisdom. The phaeton and pair would ease George's disappointment in being too young to go to town with Amelia and Charlie. The three had grown up together and the young lady's debut was bringing about the two young men's first long separation.

"You've time for a short run around the park, but see you don't keep the chaise waiting too long," Garreth called, seeing the gratitude in George's eyes. The boy had doubtless hoped to show the paces of his horses to Charlie before they left that morning.

An hour later Garreth and Charlie were seated in the private chaise as it bowled down the avenue of Elmridge. As befitted the principle seat of a marquess, the property was extensive, and under the watchful eye of Lord Tolver it had the sleek, perfectly groomed look of a profitable, well-kept estate, but the viscount was too concerned with Charlie's threat in the dining room to notice the passing scenery.

He did not for a moment believe Charlie would embarrass Lady Amelia at her ball. In the relative privacy of the two families, they would have hot words over her sudden announcement that he should do the pretty. The Earl of Wilton and his lady would join Garreth in shaking their heads in resignation while the youngsters insulted each other like two occupants of the nursery until they wore out their arguments or tea was served.

They were hardly more than grubby schoolchildren, Garreth thought as he looked over at Charlie, who was babbling along about George's new turnout. They seemed too young to be facing the stern judgement of London.

For the first time since coming to Elmridge, Garreth gave his mind over to the isolation in which Charlie had been raised. Elmridge, Salvermain, the Wilton estate and the squire's place, Golden Oaks, were all situated close to a small village, giving them a feeling of being in the centre of their area. Yet Charlie's considerable property spread north and west; Salvermain sprawled away to the south and the squire owned everything to the east for miles.

In recent years Garreth had made a point of taking Charlie with him when he went into Exeter or Plymouth on business, but visiting horse chandlers and solicitors did nothing to further the young man's knowledge of society. Thinking about the remark of the morning, he wondered if he had allowed the boy to grow to nineteen and still remain too immature to fit in. How could he have been so remiss?

Because he had been too young himself to take on the responsibilities of a surrogate father? The term rolled stiffly across his mind. Guardian, caretaker, companion at times; no term seemed to fit his relationship with his ward. Friend, older brother, uncle— those relationships suited better.

Twelve years earlier, too many changes had come into his life at one time. He had begun that winter as a bored, idle young waster, expensive and always in a scrape of some kind. Then his older brother, Albert, had succumbed to the influenza epidemic. The raging illness had also taken the sixth Marquess of Ridgeley, his wife and Charlie's nurse a mere fortnight before Albert's death.

Looking back on himself as a young buck, Garreth knew he had not been a waster by nature, but out of a lack of useful purpose. Once he involved himself in the task, he found he enjoyed the management of his own and Charlie's estates, and he liked the child. Though his relationship with his older brother had not been the best, he had been fond of Albert, and in his own sorrow he had understood the boy's grief and need for security.

Charlie had been an easy child to like. He was a gentle, amiable youngster, bright and inquisitive. He had always possessed the knack of occupying himself with any small interest at hand and was rarely dissatisfied and demanding.

Part of the fault lay in not sending him away to school, but the boy had no absorbing interest in his books. More by good fortune than design, Garreth had found an excellent tutor. Charlie had been devoted to Terry O'Hara, a well-born Irish scholar who was equally at home in the drawing room, with a fishing rod, or on the hunting field. O'Hara's ability to teach the boy to cast a fly or take a fence had commanded a respect that imbued the labour of conjugating Latin verbs with a manly aura.

Charlie's education had come to an end three months earlier when O'Hara had inherited estates of his own and returned to Ireland. The circumstance of the tutor's departure and the fact that Lady Amelia would be making her debut in society had prompted Charlie's desire to see London.

Garreth had agreed. He took a pride in Charlie's interest and knowledge of his estates, and thought he would manage well on his own when he reached his majority. Still, to be well rounded, the boy needed to enlarge his view of the world.

But that morning he had seemed so young, and society held so many snares. Garreth looked back on his own first years in town with scorn, and in later years with a sort of dismay that he could have been such a fool. Too much money and too little guidance had led him to indulge in excesses he would never condone for Charlie.

He had been led into escapades by fashionable fribbles while he had been too immature to judge the character of his friends. He gave himself a little credit for having started to change his life before the death of his brother, but he still cringed when he remembered some of his exploits.

Charlie was never going to look back on his salad days with that feeling of discomfort. Garreth would see to it that the boy went to the right places and met the right people. That meant he would also have to attend all the boring affairs he himself had successfully managed to dodge for years.

If he could get the invitations which would enable him to introduce Charlie to the right sort of people, he amended. He was the first to admit that in his younger days he had not created a desire in the matrons of society to include him in their list of invitations.

Sally. He would have to see Sally.

It would be great to see her again after so many years. His mind wandered back to the scenes of their childhood. He and Sally and . . .

He would be seeing Sally, he reminded himself. Only Sally.

CHAPTER TWO

DOROTHEA CRINGED under the lowering gaze of the resplendent footman who took her card in two fingers as if touching it might contaminate him.

"I believe I am expected," Dorothea said, mustering all the authority she was capable of at the moment. To her own ears her voice sounded a bit high and thin, as if it were trying to override the smothering influence of her appearance.

Back in Yorkshire she had been pleased with the way the brown pelisse and the green merino walking dress had lasted without showing excessive wear. Now she stood amid the opulence of wealth, and lowering her eyes, she could see it as the servant did—worn and dowdy.

Her first instincts had been correct, she decided. She should have sent her regrets when she received Sally's invitation to tea.

If she had postponed the visit for another few days she would have made a more presentable appearance, but Sally's note had been urgent, almost imperious. But then, that was just like Sally, the old Sally of their youth, with some plan or scheme which must be put forward right then.

The tone of the invitation brought back the memories of their schoolroom days with the clarity of the sting of skinned knees, breathless dashes to escape their nurses, governesses or their grooms when they went riding, and the nearly heart-bursting excitement of childish pranks and scrapes.

Dorothea could not resist accepting the invitation in the unexpressed hope of recapturing those wonderful times and renewing a friendship which had been a large part of her young world. She tried to keep her excitement from showing as the footman led the way up the stairs and opened the door of the drawing room.

"Lady Lindsterhope," he announced just as the door knocker sounded below.

"Doro!"

Dorothea felt a cool intake of a drawn breath pass her lips as she watched her hostess approach. The female who came across the room bore little resemblance to the Sally Fane of her childhood memories. Her marriage had made her a countess, Lady Jersey, who had become one of society's most powerful arbiters of fashion and deportment. Her face and carriage had stiffened to fit a firm mind and strong opinions. The style of her clothing showed the access to wealth, which often scorned and despised the less fortunate. Dorothea knew her hostess was assessing her as she approached and knew to a nicety just how she had been positioned.

Then Lady Jersey was close enough to catch Dorothea's hands in hers, and the old Sally showed in the beautiful eyes still fringed by dark lashes.

"Sally." Dorothea choked over the name, all she could get out.

"It's been *years*, but I declare, seeing you they all fall away. You look as young as ever, as if time had not touched you."

"Being here with you makes me feel they haven't," Dorothea returned. "Sixteen years since I've seen you—"

"Hush, never tell anyone there have been that many," Lady Jersey said, her laugh brittle.

Dorothea caught the insincerity of the laugh and realized Sally was listening to footsteps coming up the stairs. Her eyes were unnaturally bright as if she were in anticipation of another visitor, possibly one of some importance. Had they still been in their first youth she would have thought Sally to be planning some devilish scheme, but she let the idea drift away. They were well past games. Feeling her dowdiness more than ever Dorothea took a step backward.

"If my visit is inconvenient," she protested, entirely forgetting the invitation had come from her hostess.

"Nonsense! You'll soon see why it had to be today. Brace yourself for a grand surprise."

As the door opened Dorothea turned, steeling herself to meet she knew not whom, but prepared for the cool assessment she had seen in her friend's eyes when the visitor entered. Nothing could have prepared her for the shock of seeing the man who stood in the doorway.

"Lord Tolver," the butler announced, then stepped aside to allow the gentleman to enter and closed the doors behind him.

Dorothea clutched the back of a convenient chair and felt as if the room was spinning.

Garreth. Sixteen years fell away as if they had never existed. His face had lost the softness of youth, his skin was darker, slightly more leathery from being a great deal outdoors, but the slow smile and the grey, laughing eyes were the same. He had not yet seen her, for his attention was on their hostess. He crossed the room with the same purposeful stride she had known since her first memories when she hurried after him for the honour of carrying his fishing pole or was just allowed to tag along on his boyish adventures.

Garreth, whom she had adored as a child and dreamed of in her girlhood. She had buried those dreams and longings. After sixteen years they should have been dead, withered and turned to dust, yet just seeing him proved they had only been lying dormant. For a moment she felt as if she were unable to breathe.

Lady Jersey was moving forward, again holding out her hands.

"Garreth, it's been so long!"

He omitted a bow to catch her fingers in his grasp, his smile as wide and devilish as Dorothea remembered.

"Yes, looking at you I can see it has."

Few would have dared make such a remark to Sally Fane, and none to Lady Jersey. She was shocked into fitting the name Silence, which the ton had given her, but her surprise was shortlived.

"What an unhandsome thing to say!" She crowed with laughter. "You always were a lout."

"Don't expect any gallantry from me until you give me back my hoop," the viscount retorted, picking up on an argument that had begun a quarter of a century before.

"I did not take your hoop, much less keep it," she denied with a heat out of their childhood.

Dorothea, who had stood apart and unnoticed, had steadied her emotions, and the memory of the hoop came back with sudden clarity.

"Yes, you did, Sally," she said, contradicting her hostess. "You threw it up in the big oak tree behind our stables and we were afraid to climb up after it."

"Doro, don't be such a rattle! You promised never to tell."

"I did promise! I'm sorry, I forgot."

The viscount turned toward Doro, his face a study in surprise that held for an instant before his sardonic grin turned enquiring and then softened in pleasure.

"Doro?" He crossed the short distance in two strides and greatly surprised the second guest by ignoring her hands and giving her a sound embrace before stepping back for a close look at her.

"Sweet Doro," he murmured, the light of remembered friendship in his eyes.

"A surprise for both of you," Lady Jersey said, her own face alight. "One for me, too, hearing from both of you within the same week, and discovering you were both in London."

The door opened again to admit the butler and two footmen bringing in tea, and the conversation was put off until they were alone again. The viscount was still gazing at Dorothea as if he could not believe she was there.

"I'm so surprised," he said. "It was as if you had dropped off the earth."

"I know," Lady Jersey agreed. "For the longest time I heard nothing from her, though I had written, but I suppose your grief made writing difficult."

Garreth opened his mouth as if to speak and then closed it. A man of thirty-five would hate to be reminded of writing the letter he had sent her after her father's death. Reading it years later, she had seen it as his youthful and unfocused desire to aid her in a time of trouble. She did not consider his offer of marriage as the ardour of a lover, but the fondness of a lifelong friend.

Dorothea started to nod, at first accepting the excuse Sally gave her, but then she thought better of it.

"Later I learned that you both wrote, but in the confusion of my father's death and the sudden move back to the country, the letters were somehow misplaced. They weren't found until years later."

The truth was far less pleasant. Her brother had kept from her the condolences and expressions of support sent by her friends, fearing they might in some way interfere with his plans for her to make a wealthy marriage. Five years later, after his death, his son had found the letters and sent them to her.

"You married Lindsterhope," the viscount said slowly. "A bit loose in the haft, I heard." Suddenly he seemed to recall he was speaking to the baron's widow. "Sorry, old girl."

"My late husband was a gentleman," Dorothea said firmly. "He was generous and kind, until a stroke disordered his mind. His grandson, Tom, will reach his majority in November, and we will be nicely circumstanced."

"Sweet Doro, you deserved better," Garreth said. "In November... But in the meantime how shall you go along?"

She smiled. "Carefully. We were intending to wait until next year before coming to town, but...." Dorothea twisted her fingers and her soft features took on a look of discomfort. "I could be mistaken, but I think there is a gentleman in our neighbourhood with designs on Tom's fortune, and I felt the need to remove him from that influence."

"An ivory-turner?" Garreth asked, thinking of the snares he had invisioned Charlie falling into. Young men were often led to lose vast amounts of money by making friends with fashionable fellows who took them to dishonest gaming houses and later received a share of the losses.

Dorothea shook her head. "I almost wish the gentleman were, because Tom has no serious interest in cards or dice. If my suspicions are correct, this person hopes to lure or trap Tom into offering for his sister. He attempted to attach Farrie, but she is afraid of him. I'm heartily grateful for that."

"And the boy?" Garreth asked. "Has he any suspicion?"

"No, and warning him will do no good," Dorothea said. "His grandfather was bedridden when Tom was four, and he's never had the fatherly attentions a boy needs. He is devoted to Sir— To this man and would not believe it." She raised imploring eyes to Lord Tolver. "He's had no one but Farrie and me for so long. He's wanted so much to be a part of the world he reads about. He's never thought of himself as a person of means who could be used because of his wealth or position.''

''You'll have to watch him carefully,'' Garreth said. ''It's unfortunate that he hasn't been exposed to more of society before now.''

It was not wonderful that Lady Jersey, well aware of her fame in the social world, felt no need to bring either of her old friends up to date on her activities. Instead she turned to the viscount.

''You dropped out of sight as suddenly as Doro,'' she said.

''You know what I've been up to,'' Garreth said. ''I've written to you.''

''Four letters in twelve years.'' Lady Jersey smiled. ''You were always an admirable correspondent.''

''I don't know what you've been up to,'' Dorothea said, prompting the conversation.

''It was right after he ascended to the title,'' Lady Jersey explained. ''I expected him to go on the strut after the purse strings fell into his hands, but he surprised me.''

''And myself, as well.'' Garreth smiled, thinking of how he'd once boasted of what his life would be if he had the wherewithal his brother possessed. To give him due credit, he had never once thought of wishing himself in his brother's place.

''With Charlie, his holdings and my own to look after, there's never been any time to indulge in more fanciful pastimes.''

''Charlie?'' Dorothea asked, not recognizing the name.

''Marquess of Ridgeley, Charles . . . ?'' Lady Jersey gazed at the viscount, her brows raised in enquiry.

"Landruth," Garreth supplied.

Lady Jersey shook her head as if mystified.

"I never believed there was the least harm in you, Garreth, but you didn't appear to be guardian material. I never understood how his father could have left the boy in your care."

"He didn't. He appointed my brother. The late marquess died a fortnight before Albert, and not knowing a guardianship couldn't be inherited, Albert told me I was to take on the boy if he didn't make it. I didn't know, either, not for ten years."

"Good heavens!" Lady Jersey looked startled. "Did they catch you up?"

Garreth shrugged. "Looked like a good idea to acquire some property abutting Elmridge. When it came time to register the deeds, I had to prove my right to contract for the estate." He shrugged and grinned. "No trouble. The court looked over the estate records and decided to affirm me legally. Now I can thrash the brat with impunity."

"You probably do," Lady Jersey said, shaking her head.

"Of course he doesn't." Dorothea spoke up, stern in her defence of the viscount. Her role had always been to defend one of her friends against the barbs of the other. She was falling back into the old habit.

"I would quick enough if there were a need," Garreth corrected. "But he's a pretty decent little sprig. Not so small anymore. Nineteen two months ago, and as wild as a young colt."

"And are we going to have him kicking up larks all over town?" Lady Jersey asked, pouring more tea for Doro.

"Not if I can help it. I'm going to keep him on a leash until he knows his way around. That's why I need your help," he said, grinning at Sally.

"I do not walk young men on leashes," she retorted.

"No, but you can see I get the invitations to the right places so he meets the right people, and you owe it to me."

Lady Jersey's eyes narrowed.

"Why do I owe it to you?"

The viscount grinned.

"Because you never gave me back my hoop."

CHAPTER THREE

ON A SUNNY AFTERNOON a week after Dorothea's visit to Berkeley Square, the Sailings were gathered in the drawing room of Lindsterhope House on Green Street. Tom was sitting at the escritoire, laboriously working on a letter to the aging and somewhat inept bailiff of Marvale.

"'...and the new calves must be kept in the barn by the lower pasture until all danger of frost is past...' Can you think of anything else to add, Doro?"

"I think you've mentioned everything of importance," she answered, then smiled at his sigh of relief as he set about recopying his letter.

The young Baron of Lindsterhope had never been bookish, and his normal handwriting was an almost illegible scrawl, but knowing the shifts to which Dorothea and Farrie were being put in order to create a suitable wardrobe, he had manfully taken over the chore of the family correspondence.

Back in Yorkshire, Dorothea's legacy from Cousin Margaret had seemed a fortune, but they had quickly discovered the cost of maintaining a house in town, where everything had to be purchased, would soon make alarming inroads into their small capital.

They immediately gave up any idea of refurbishing the house. Out-of-date furniture, put in storage years

ago, had been brought down from the lumber rooms
and stood backed against the walls or tentatively near
the hearth like strangers trying to find footing in new
surroundings.

The second step in their plan which had to be aban-
doned had been the numerous trips to fashionable
modistes. Bond Street had seen far less of their cus-
tom than had Grafton House, where muslins, silks,
trims and ribbons could be purchased by the yard and
made up at home. Fortunately both Farrie and Dorothea, as well as their maids, were accomplished with
the needle, and Dorothea had a deft hand at cutting
patterns.

But though they were unable to enjoy the privileges
of unrestrained spending, they had no concern over
appearing dowdy. In Yorkshire they had worked industriously on lengths of intricate embroidery, planning for the time their careful work would trim new
and fashionable clothing. They had brought the re-
sults of their efforts with them in hopes of buying
lengths of fabrics to match, and they had begun to do
so far more quickly than they'd expected. Farrie was
even then adding a ruffle of white muslin trimmed
with a border of embroidered green leaves to a green-
and-white sprigged muslin gown. When finished it
would bear all the signs of having been purchased on
Bond Street.

Their expenditures for ready-made items had been
strictly limited to bonnets, slippers and reticules, those
items their busy needles could not provide.

The one expenditure that could not be reduced was
Tom's clothing. When he understood their financial
problems, he had instantly offered to return home,

thereby avoiding the need to provide a wardrobe for him. He was set on leaving town, and would have done so had Dorothea not pleaded that his presence was necessary for both her comfort and Farrie's. She could not tell him *he* was the reason for the trip, and Farrie had shed tears before he could be convinced to take himself to the best tailors and procure the necessary outfits to squire them about town.

He conceded when it was presented to him that to go to less than the best might mean accepting inferior raiment, necessitating costly replacement. His first foray into the streets of Mayfair had convinced him to hie himself to the tailor, and he had kept to the house until a trickle of deliveries put him in possession of suitable attire.

But if the aspect was bleak, the atmosphere was not. Dorothea had been long used to living on the borders of exigency, and the younger members of the family could remember nothing else. They all possessed sunny natures and had learned to take their pleasure from the little things in life.

On this particular afternoon they felt wealthy indeed. Tom was resplendent in a new broadcloth coat, unmistakably of Weston cut, pale grey pantaloons and new Hessian boots. Much to Tom's surprise and delight, Anthony, who served both as footman and Tom's valet, had managed to put a shine on the new boots equal to any beau in society.

The ladies were attired in afternoon walking dresses, having decided to take the air later. The small embroidered flowers trimming Farrie's pale blue dress, and the velvet ribbon trimming Dorothea's wine-coloured kerseymere gave them the feeling of being in the first stare of fashion.

They were occupying themselves while waiting for their visitors. Dorothea had explained how she knew Viscount Tolver.

"Sweet Doro, you're not telling all!" Farrie Sailings exclaimed, having caught Dorothea's hesitation when she had spoken of Garreth. She looked up from the ruffle she was sewing with tiny, perfect stitches. Her dark eyes twinkled with mischief.

Tom had been mending the nib of a pen at the escritoire taking care to protect his new clothing, but he turned, his face alight with the desire to tease.

"Are you keeping secrets?" He rose and sauntered over to stand behind his sister, looking across at Dorothea.

Both ladies were busily stitching a dress for Farrie. Tom watched them at their work, and when his sister was busy rethreading her needle, he slid his hand down the back of the confidante and eased a thin, ruffled pillow toward her, covering her pin cushion.

"I'm certainly not keeping secrets," Dorothea answered, her own head bent over the embroidered strip that would become the waistband on Farrie's dress. Both Tom and Farrie had caught the check in her explanation of how she had met Lord Tolver again. The hesitation had come about because of the reason for the meeting, not any reticence in explaining that they had been childhood playmates. She'd had the week since the meeting at Lady Jersey's to come to terms with her emotions.

And she had needed the time. Seeing him again had brought her girlhood dreams to life like a seed that had found new soil and water. She had lectured herself; she would encounter him often during the season. He would be across the room at parties and at Almack's, since he had voiced his decision to see that his ward become familiar with society and its traps before he turned the boy loose on the town.

She must accept the idea of seeing females throw out lures to him. He was thirty-five, viewed by some as an excellent age for marriage. Hopeful mamas would be attracted to his fortune, while his strong good looks and slow provocative smile would set young girls' hearts to palpitating.

She had been assiduous in warning herself she must give up any idea of attaching his notice. Her lack of success in convincing herself had been apparent to her only that morning when she received a message from him. The elation she felt when a footman had appeared at the door with a twisted note and the instruction to wait for an answer was that of a woman still in love. The message had been short and terse.

Doro,
When are we invited to tea? Want to bring Charlie to meet Tom.

Garreth

No words of Lord Byron's could have been sweeter. The lack of social courtesies indicated Garreth had picked up their relationship where it had been interrupted years ago. The feelings he'd had for her had undergone no change. She knew better than to believe they were as affectionate as hers, but at least time had not destroyed what had existed.

She invited him for that very afternoon.

"A marquess," Farrie murmured, looking up from her sewing. The laughter left her eyes. "Will he be starched and stuffy, do you think?" She looked anxiously around the shabby room.

Dorothea glanced up and read the lurking doubts in the two pairs of dark eyes regarding her. They were facing the age-old difficulties of all young people when they first stepped out into a widening world. Though neither would have admitted it, they were a little frightened of society.

"I shouldn't think so," Dorothea said slowly. "Lord Tolver knows what is due his ward's rank, but he was never a stickler on form."

The clanging of the knocker brought a halt to their ruminations, and all three looked toward the door apprehensively.

"We'll soon f-find out," Tom said, his stutter making a lie of his affected nonchalance.

"Tom!" Farrie hissed, suddenly cramming her sewing into her basket and thrusting it at him.

He took the handle, started toward the cabinet which stood between the two front windows and then whirled back to reach for Dorothea's work. With both baskets, he strode across the room, jerked open the doors and thrust them inside. He had just shut them away and turned back to join the ladies when the door to the hall was thrust open and the footman, puffed to his fullest, gave the names of the visitors in ringing accents.

"Lady Amelia Easterly, Lord Ridgeley, Lord Tolver."

Dorothea's elation faded into a cold emptiness by the entrance of the young lady on Garreth's arm. She was young, hardly older than Farrie, though taller. Her gold ringlets framed a face both aristocratic and beautiful.

A cold beauty, Dorothea thought. She carried herself as if she knew her own worth. She was exquisitely dressed in a pale blue muslin trimmed with darker blue grosgrain ribbons; matching ribbons trimmed her hat of woven straw. The stiffness of her features conveyed an impression of disapproval of her surroundings. She would freeze all natural response in Tom and Farrie, who were already shy and nervous and all too willing to draw back into their shells.

Lord Ridgeley, too, was stiff, giving the lie to Dorothea's assurances to Tom and Farrie that he would not be stuffy, and his demeanour was bringing out in Tom an effort to appear just as formal.

Dorothea stepped forward and held out her hand. In her desire to ease the tension she spoke too rapidly. "Garreth—Lord Tolver—may I introduce...." Her step-grandchildren sounded ridiculous when she was only four and thirty. "Lord Lindsterhope and Miss Sailings."

The introductions proceeded with grave formality, though Dorothea thought she could see a twinkle in Lord Tolver's eyes.

Farrie, sensible of her responsibility to entertain a young woman so near her own age, led Lady Amelia over to the confidante, and the two younger gentleman followed. They were moving awkwardly, trying to give way to each other in an excess of courtesy.

Dorothea watched them go and ached for Farrie and Tom. After living such reclusive existences, they were dreadfully unsure of themselves, seeing everyone around them as having more knowledge of how to go on than they. The last people they needed to meet were Lady Amelia and Lord Ridgeley, with their perfect attire and high-nosed dignity.

Farrie offered Lady Amelia a seat and the young lady lowered herself to the confidante, but she was not nearly settled before she gave out a squeal and leapt to her feet again.

"My pincushion!" Farrie gasped, her face turning scarlet as she picked up the offending article. "I'm so sorry, I don't know how...." Her explanation failed her.

Tom stepped forward at once and removed the object from his sister's hand.

"My—my f-fault entirely. A rig—a joke on m'sister. Didn't mean to l-leave it...." His gallant assumption of the guilt dissolved into confusion, his own face turning crimson. He held the pincushion as if he didn't know how to dispose of it, and looked appealingly in Dorothea's direction, but for once she was stunned beyond coming to his rescue.

"A rig..." muttered Lady Amelia, her displeasure evident. She ignored both the Sailings as she turned to the young marquess.

"Charlie, *you* put him up to it," she accused. "Don't you *dare* deny it."

"I jolly well wish I *had* after what you did to me yesterday," he retorted and turned to Tom, all his assumed dignity falling away. "Half the fun is letting a fellow in on a thing before it happens," he said, his tone full of injury.

"My heavens, so unfortunate," Dorothea said, and looked up at Lord Tolver. "I hope Lady Amelia doesn't develop a distaste for us."

"More likely she'll gore Charlie with one of those pins before the tea tray arrives," the viscount answered, taking Dorothea's arm and leading her toward the end of the room. He gave a sudden low chuckle.

"Best thing that could have happened. It put a stop to their playacting."

"Playacting?" Dorothea looked back over her shoulder to see the four young people settling down, the young ladies on the confidante and Tom arranging the chairs for himself and the marquess.

"Don't you remember how we were when we first came to town?" Tolver smiled down at her as he led her toward the windows where two chairs were placed in easy conversational proximity, separated by a small marquetry table.

"One week we were careering all over the countryside," he went on, "and the next we were in London, trying to appear more polished than the rest of society combined. We weren't even sure what polish was."

Dorothea smiled at the memory and nodded. "I was frightened to death."

"Terrified you'd say the wrong thing, spill something or trip over a carpet." He sat back and lazily watched the young people as they warmed to each other.

"I hope I didn't put you out by bringing Amelia," he said. He explained the close friendship between her and Charlie. "She doesn't have a female friend in town."

Dorothea looked over at the quartet close to the fireplace. Lady Amelia and the marquess bore little resemblance to the dignified young people who had entered the room. The lovely blonde was busily abusing the marquess, raising her voice slightly as he tried to override her with hot denials and counteraccusations. Tom and Farrie had lost their shyness and were adding their bits, wrangling with each other as they vied to keep apace in the swapping of exploits.

"I'm glad you did," Dorothea said warmly. "Farrie is on the brink of drawing back, though I will say Sally has been so helpful in getting us invitations. From next week forward, our calendar will be crowded. Perhaps next year we can do some entertaining, but...." She waved her hand, indicating the condition of the house. "I hadn't thought it would be so...bad," she finished lamely.

"That's twice you've mentioned next year with enthusiasm," Garreth said. He had let his head fall back on the antimacassar, but beneath his lowered lashes his eyes gleamed with keen perception.

Dorothea shifted in her chair. "It's so odious. There's no lack of funds, but my late husband tied everything up in a trust until Tom reaches his majority in November. Tom's made so many plans, but left to his own devices, he will be sensible, I think. If I can just keep him away from the influence of...that friend of his." She shied away from mentioning Sir Gerald by name. She had no proof he was an adventurer, and it was not in her character to malign a person who might possibly be innocent.

"I can understand a trust for the boy, but do you mean to tell me Lindsterhope didn't provide for you?"

Garreth's question was too blunt, too accusing for Dorothea not to make some defence.

"He was ill, you see, and I am persuaded that in his deluded thinking, he was giving me the honour of his complete trust. He wanted me to take care of Tom and Farrie, and by withholding all but the barest stipend until Tom comes of age, he was protecting me from fortune-hunters and the children from being influenced by them."

"Still..."

"The trustees have been diligent in making the most of our invested funds. In ten months we will be able to command all the elegancies of life. That's where the danger lies for Tom, I think. Left to himself, he will restore Marvale, this house and see to it that Farrie's dowry is considerably enlarged. Beyond that he has no grandiose ideas of his own. I'm just afraid other people will put unwise thoughts into his head."

"He sounds like a fine young man," Garreth said.

"I cannot conceive of a better," Dorothea said warmly. "Only, he can be easily influenced by people he trusts. It's important that he learn that not everyone who seems honourable is so."

"You're wise," Garreth said.

"That's why Cousin Margaret's legacy was so welcome right now, and it was certainly a surprise. I'd not seen the woman twice in my life."

"Relatives." Garreth grimaced at the word. "You were fortunate with your cousin. I could wish Amelia's parents such a pleasant surprise, rather than the trouble they're going through just now."

"It must be hard to cope with problems in the family when they are trying to bring out a daughter," Dorothea answered, not sure what he meant, but since good manners forbade enquiry, she said no more.

"Harry—that's Lady Harriet, Amelia's mother—was raised by her great-aunt, Lady Cynthia Hardston. Of late the old woman's turned jealous and suspicious—age, I suppose. She's kicking up a dust, insisting she's ready to stick her spoon in the wall and demanding Harry return to Salvermain. Nothing but a snit because of Amelia's season, if you ask me. Still, it's throwing Harry and John into a stew. It's not what she leaves, though she's pretty well fixed—Harry still remembers her kindnesses."

"John," Dorothea mused, having connected two names that gave her a glimmer of knowledge. "John Easterly, the Earl of Wilton?"

Garreth nodded. "Close neighbours of ours at Elmridge."

"Surely they must have friends and relatives in town who could take Lady Amelia even if Lady Harriet had to leave?"

Garreth shook his head. "Family thin on the tree, and they've stayed pretty much to themselves."

"Lady Amelia wasn't sent away to a seminary?"

"No, she's just like Charlie, she wouldn't go, and Lord and Lady Wilton liked having her at home. You wouldn't think it to look at her, but she's as fine a judge of horseflesh as any man in the country. When push comes to shove, she'll take some blockheaded sportsman and give him the finest stables in England."

"No, I wouldn't think it," Dorothea said, turning her gaze to the blond aristocratic beauty. "When she first arrived I thought she was ... was ..."

"Pretty high in the instep?" Garreth finished for her, his eyes alight with laughter. "Terrified is a better description. She knows you're a friend of Sally's. Good job she sat on that pincushion and broke her reserve. Beneath that thin veneer of dignity she's a young scamp, no more ready for marriage than Charlie."

Dorothea could not see herself as an object of fright, but she could readily understand the nervousness that brought on a stiff demeanour.

"I remember how frightened I was when I began my first season, and I had you and Sally."

"And me with only two females to fall back on," he said, and realizing he'd been maladroit, added, "not that I could have found two I'd trust more, but a young blade needs his own set."

Dorothea nodded. "Tom does. We've lived such a quiet life in Yorkshire." She looked over at him, her memories of her first season coming back with a sudden disconcerting clarity. "Not all young men are as nervous and awkward. You weren't."

"Oh, wasn't I?" Garreth laughed softly, the sort of rueful chuckle associated with old memories.

"But you couldn't have been. I remember my first visit to Almack's. You were there. You had such polish, such address, I was half afraid of you. I remember thinking we had been riding in the country just a fortnight before, yet you seemed so different, so poised and at home among all those strangers."

He gave her a slow, lazy smile. "Wonder what lion of fashion I was aping that night?"

She was shocked at his admission. "You always appeared to be so sure of yourself." Dorothea ducked her head to hide her blush as he turned a laughing gaze on her. She was saying too much. She was letting her heart control her tongue.

"Sweet Doro, you should have told me so then. No, it's better that you didn't. I might have been so set up in my own esteem I would have made an even greater fool of myself than I managed to do anyway."

"You didn't." She could not stop the denial.

"All young blades do," he answered, with a tinge of bitterness. "If there's no one to give them a hint, they invariably ape the wrong people and later regret it. That's why I'm keeping an eye on Charlie."

"He won't resent being led about?" Dorothea tried to imagine someone managing Garreth's affairs when he was first on the town, but she could not.

"No, because I'll take him to all the places I would rather he never went, as well as all the places he should go. I don't intend to shield him or set his limits, but if it's not pointed out to him he'll suffer before he learns what to avoid."

Dorothea was not sure she understood what Garreth meant by places Charlie should not go. She knew enough about the world to know there was a side of men's lives about which a well-bred female did not enquire.

Since they were stepping close to a subject that was best avoided, she was relieved when the drawing-room door opened. The footman entered carrying a well-loaded tea tray. He was followed by the butler who brought a tiered wicker stand laden with plates of sandwiches, scones and cakes.

Tom, with the energy and appetite of youth, rose to push a table forward. Charlie, by now thoroughly at home, moved to help, while Lady Amelia ordered the young marquess about and Farrie gave suggestions. The butler, an old retainer of the Lindsterhope household, was accustomed to the jolly wrangling of the brother and sister, but the footman was new to the household and so stood stiffly, as if expecting the young gentlemen to knock the tray from his hands in their efforts to get the table where they wanted it.

"Best stir yourself, or the tea will be on the carpet," the viscount said, rising and offering a hand to Doro.

"I noticed you are not much put out by their antics," she said as they crossed the room.

"There's not an ounce of harm in the whole thundering herd," the viscount said. He stepped forward to deftly retrieve a small lacquered chest from Tom who was handing it to Charlie, seemingly unaware he had already loaded his guest with a large floral arrangement and a china figurine.

"Careful, you young thatchgallows, or you'll have it all on the floor."

Dorothea's gaze flew to Tom's face, not knowing what his reaction would be. He had never been spoken to in the viscount's forthright but casual style, but to her relief, Tom just grinned and moved back to allow the footman to place the tray.

In a more formal atmosphere the six people who'd gathered for tea might have pretended to hardly notice the offering, but the contretemps following the arrival of the guests had put the party on a comfortable footing.

While Dorothea poured out, Farrie passed round the small plates and then a platter of sandwiches, offering them first to Lady Amelia.

"Do take one quickly, else Tom will scoff them all," she said.

"One for each of us," Amelia returned, slipping one on Farrie's plate and taking one for herself.

"I think it's time to retaliate," Tom told Charlie, grabbing up a plate of buttered scones from the tiered rack.

"Shall we join forces, also?" Charlie helped himself and started to load Tom's plate when the viscount reached out and caught his ward's wrist.

"Not so fast, you bottomless pit."

In a sudden and unexpected move, Dorothea reached forward and nipped a scone off the plate held by Tom and guarded from above by the strong arms of Tolver and Charlie.

"Doro!" Tom ejaculated with a surprised laugh.

"I haven't lost my touch, after all," she said smugly as she placed the scone on her plate and resumed pouring the tea.

"So this is a society tea," Charlie said, taking his cup and looking toward his guardian. "Not so different from at home."

"I can't wait to see Doro pull that trick in Almack's," Garreth said, giving her a sardonic grin.

"I say, will be you going to Almack's tomorrow night?" Tom asked Charlie. "Doro and Farrie are." He paused, assuming a nonchalance. "I might as well tag along."

Charlie threw a questioning look at his guardian.

"We are," Lady Amelia said. "If Uncle Garreth doesn't want to go you can come with us."

The marquess cast another look at the viscount who was in the process of holding his cup for more tea. Lady Amelia, less patient with her longtime friend than she was with the others, frowned at him.

"Charlie, do you come with us?" she asked. "You can't want Uncle Garreth to come along and hold your hand."

"Can't I just!" Charlie retorted, and then looked aghast when he realized what he had said. His cheeks brightened as he dropped his eyes to his plate. "Well, not precisely," he muttered, his face scarlet before he turned the attack, taking the emphasis off himself. "I doubt I'll see you an inch away from your mother's skirts."

"No, I shouldn't think so," Dorothea put in, trying to soothe what might become an argument. "When one first goes into society, one would like the guidance of someone more knowledgeable. It makes one feel much safer."

Charlie's artless gaff had had a profound effect on the other three young people, who did not know how to express their sympathy with the spirit of his remark. With the gallantry of his generous nature, Tom made an effort.

"It does make sense," he said, nodding slowly as if giving the matter serious thought. "Lots of things a fellow might need to be warned of. Might not think or know to ask about in advance. Wouldn't mind a hint here and there myself."

Dorothea busied herself with tea things on the tray, straightening the row of extra silver spoons and adjusting the pot which was already sufficiently near at hand. Tom's offhand announcement was trilling through her head. She had been trying to rid herself of the hope of seeing more of Garreth than a fleeting glance across a room. If he were to take Tom seriously, her opportunities would be greatly multiplied.

"Lord," Garreth said, sighing and putting his cup aside, "who would have thought I was destined to be a bear leader to a couple of budding rank riders?"

"I call that jolly," Charlie said, feeling he had been vindicated in his thoughtless admission. "Come along with us, Tom. Then we'll have someone to talk to while we're standing around between turns of doing the pretty."

"Much pretty I can see from you two," Garreth muttered, watching Tom and Charlie divide the last of the cake between them.

"Did you ask Lady Lindsterhope about walking in the park?" Charlie asked the viscount.

Farrie at once gave it as her opinion that a walk after tea was just what she would most like, and Tom joined in, saying he thought it a grand idea. Garreth turned his head to the hostess.

"The beasts have taken it into their heads to stroll in the park. The thing is, society might not recognize my avuncular standing."

"My maid came with me in the carriage," Lady Amelia explained, "but Uncle Garreth says he won't take us to the park without a more acceptable chaperon."

"Nothing like letting one feel one is welcome for her own sake," the viscount said, raising one sardonic eyebrow.

"Lord, Amelia, mind your tongue," Charlie broke in. "We want Lady Lindsterhope to come because we want her company, so won't you please come, if you would be so kind?"

Dorothea nodded, her placid expression hiding a far deeper pleasure, and she hardly heard Lady Amelia's pretty apology for her maladroit remark. She reminded herself Garreth was deeply interested in the young people. Seeing them gain their footing in society was more important to him than her company, but after sixteen years of existing without a dream or a hope in her heart, she could not persuade her emotions to let go of their tenuous fantasy.

"So fortunate that Farrie and I had dressed for just such an outing," she said. "We will just get our hats."

When the ladies ascended to the upper floor to prepare for the outing, Lady Amelia accompanied Farrie to her room. From her own room, Dorothea could hear the young ladies chattering as if they had been lifelong acquaintances. She could hear in their muted voices the rush of confidences, the reaching out of youth lonely for a kindred spirit, and sighed for the old closeness she'd had with Sally at a similar age. The old feelings were still there, but life tended to intrude, and those happy, artless times were lost under the pressure of maturity.

So many pressures, she thought, turning her mind to the bonnet she had taken from its box. She had meant to keep the gay confection of straw and bright green ribbons for a different occasion, for a time later

in the season when she would need a freshening of her
wardrobe. The legacy would only go so far, and who
knew what sudden and unexpected expenses might
need to be met.

She sighed, started to replace the hat in the box and
then decided against it. With firm steps she marched
to the mirror and tied the bright ribbons under her
chin with firm sure movements. Who knew how often
she would have the opportunity to stroll with Garreth?

She tugged on her gloves, picked up her reticule and
a light parasol and left the room. She could only live
one day at a time. The idyll could come to an end soon
enough.

At the top of the stairs she paused, gazing down into
the hall. In the doorway of the drawing room the
footman stood with the heavy tea tray forgotten in his
hands. The scene he was watching had overridden his
training and his face held a wide grin.

In the hallway, three fashionable gentlemen were
poised, wearing their curly-brimmed beavers at rak-
ish angles, their walking sticks in their gloved hands.
The younger gentlemen were easily recognized by their
slimmer shoulders. At some unspoken command they
stepped forward, flourishing their walking sticks.

"A little less swagger with the stick, Charlie, or
you'll trip up Tom." A slight tremor of laughter softened the viscount's order, and from above, the shaking of his shoulders was apparent as the younger
gentlemen swaggered about the hall in a playful bur-
lesque of a fashionable stroll.

Dorothea was too sensible to believe the viscount
was giving the young gentlemen instruction. They were

occupying their time and their high spirits with some foolish pretence, harmless enough, since they were within doors with no one to see but the footman. In keeping with the tolerance he had showed at tea, Garreth was watching them, letting them go their limit.

"I'm impressed," Dorothea called as she started down the stairs. "Shall I perfect the art of twirling my parasol in order to be in such fashionable company?"

"No, hold yourself in readiness to act as a proper chaperon," the viscount said, his eyes twinkling. "If they start their antics in the park, we'll push them under a passing carriage."

"With aplomb," Dorothea added.

"With poise and aplomb," the viscount amended, removing his hat while they waited for the younger ladies to join them.

CHAPTER FOUR

WHEN DOROTHEA ENTERED the hallowed portals of
Almack's on the following evening, she was pleased
with the appearance of her wards, knowing they had
nothing to blush about regarding the impression they
would make on the society gathering.

In a well-cut coat, satin knee breeches and striped
stockings, Tom was as finely dressed as any gentleman attending, and moreover, though he was not
overly tall, his slender, but well-knit physique showed
off his clothing to perfection.

Farrie's quick needle had fashioned tiny pink ro-
settes and delicate leaves from lengths of pink and
green satin ribbon, and her white muslin gown was
trimmed at the bottom with alternating rows of each.
A rosebush in the garden, which had miraculously
survived the neglect of Lindsterhope House, had provided two blossoms now secured by a green ribbon in
her hair. They added just the right touch of colour to
bring out the blush of excitement in her cheeks.

As a chaperon, Dorothea could indulge her fancy
for darker colours, and in Grafton House she had
discovered a deep emerald-green silk which lent itself
perfectly to black velvet ruching and a row of covered
buttons. She had suffered some qualms over the expense of the dress, and her penchant for honesty

would not let her deny she was taking more than average care in her appearance because of her renewed acquaintance with Garreth.

She had steeled herself to bear the disappointment of not having his company, though she knew he meant to be present, so she was mildly surprised and quite pleased to see him crossing the room, his goal obviously the Sailings party. He had not quite reached them when Dorothea noticed the tightness around his mouth.

"Come and meet Harry," he said when the amenities of greeting were barely finished. "Charlie and Amelia are standing like two blocks and don't know what to do with themselves."

Though Dorothea had meant to pause and speak to Sally, she was too pleased to find Garreth watching for her to demur. There was nothing loverlike in his greeting, however. His interest in her company was rooted in his desire to see the young people made more comfortable, yet his assumption that she would fall in with his plans just as she always had when they were children was to Dorothea a promising sign.

She allowed him to lead her into the next and much larger room, where musicians were playing a country dance. Since the season was just beginning the rooms were not crowded, and without any to-do the viscount led her toward a small sofa where a high-nosed matron in blue satin sat with Lady Amelia. The young marquess stood behind the sofa as if on guard, though his expression changed to a smile when he saw the Sailings.

"A pair of young turnips," Garreth muttered under his breath. "Maybe seeing Tom and Farrie will put some life into them."

Dorothea suppressed a sigh. But what did she expect? Concern for the young people drew him to her. She hadn't any right to expect more.

Lady Amelia rose from the confidante and offered her place to Dorothea when the introductions were made. Dorothea wasn't sure she wanted to join Lady Harriet, who lowered her brows and frowned, her eagle eyes glinting.

"From Yorkshire," Lady Harriet remarked, as if summing up Doro's character from her origins.

"Yes, Marvale is east of Gainsborough," Dorothea conceded, wondering just what the admission would convey to the stiff-backed woman.

"At least you know butter doesn't grow on a bush," Lady Harriet snapped. "Can't abide these city hen-wits." With that sweeping comment she sat back, looking more relaxed and stared out across the room as if, having done her social duty, no more needed to be said.

Dorothea felt as winded as if she had run a race or passed some other exhaustive test, but apparently she had passed it. Since Lady Harriet laid no further claim on her attention, she turned her head to see what had become of Tom and Farrie.

Farrie was standing with Lord Tolver and Lady Amelia, who was telling them some long and involved story accompanied by a lot of gesturing. The shyness that usually cloaked the dark-haired girl's beauty was absent as she enjoyed Amelia's liveliness and Garreth's casual avuncular attitude.

Beyond them, Tom and Charlie had their heads together as they discussed what must be a matter of great import. By looking in the direction of their frequent gazes, Dorothea noticed a young lady of striking beauty. A nonpareil, she thought, taking in the honey-gold hair and the blue sprigged muslin with a shower of darker bows which doubtless matched her eyes. But the young lady's stance was a bit too perfect, the angle of her chin too high, and there was a naturalness to her hauteur which warned Dorothea she was not putting on a stiff demeanour to hide her unease.

Dorothea's protective feelings for Tom cried out for her to warn him to be careful, but even then it was too late. He and Charlie had started in the blonde's direction, strolling casually, but clearly making her their aim.

"Charlie's a fool," Lady Harriet spoke up, tapping Dorothea on the hand with her fan and nodding in the beauty's direction. "That Kettling chit won't waste any time on him or your boy. No point in it."

Dorothea stiffened as she took Lady Harriet's remark to be a disparagement about Tom, though she had not yet ascertained whether it was a slur on his birth or fortune. Not even for Garreth's sake could she allow her charges to be maligned.

"Tom has no need to court wealth," she said, her voice exceedingly cool.

"But the Kettling girl does," Lady Harriet replied. "Drat. There's that Vinnie Arsdale waving at me. Silly goose of a woman, but I suppose Amelia should be seen at her niece's ball. Have to do my duty by my girl." Having given her reason, she rose abruptly and started through the crowd to cross the room.

Another dance was forming, and it was not surprising that two such attractive young ladies as Lady Amelia and Farrie were solicited to take the floor. Dorothea was for the moment caught up in meeting the Honourable Mr. Nelson, a starched young sprig whose collar would not allow him to see the floor within five feet of where he stood. Lady Amelia's eyes twinkled so wickedly that Dorothea was half-tempted to do her implied duty to Lady Harriet and keep Amelia with her rather than risk some scrape.

Lord Farling was a nervous young man with the bright complexion of country life and so reminded her of Tom that she had no qualms of seeing Farrie take the floor with him.

As the two couples moved off toward the forming sets, Garreth sat down beside Doro.

"Well, that's two of them fairly started," he said and turned his head to give Dorothea a grin, reminiscent of all their young escapades, yet on his more mature face it also carried a sensuous promise she was sure was unintentional.

"The first public dance was the worst, remember?"

His attention was suddenly diverted and Dorothea knew from the direction of his gaze that he was watching the encounter between Charlie, Tom and the Kettling beauty. She turned her head and was just in time to see Tom's shoulders slump. The movement was slight, probably not even noticeable to Garreth, but characteristic of Tom when he had been disappointed or hurt. Charlie was abruptly turning away, his face diffused with colour.

"Damn that high-priced piece of market—your pardon, Doro—but just because they know they can't get their hooks in Charlie is no reason to snub the young rascals."

Doro's eyes widened, her sympathy for the boys momentarily pushed aside by her surprise.

"You didn't tell Lord Kettling that to his face, did you?"

"Not in so many words. I just let it be known at White's that as long as I hold the purse strings, Charlie has to have my consent, and he's too young to be considered fair game."

"Good heavens! Your only recourse is to call Lord Kettling out for the insult."

Garreth gave her a sharp look before his shoulder shook in a suppressed laugh.

"In that case you must call Lady Kettling out. Would you like the use of one of my gloves? I don't think those lace things you're wearing will have quite the right effect." He sobered. "But you're saying I'm too protective."

"No, just too..." How could she say what she felt? "I'm persuaded we're both reliving our first fears and experiences through them. They have to suffer some of the pains we went through, don't you think? Though I confess I would positively relish giving Lady Kettling a setdown."

She felt the force of Garreth's entire attention as she received another of those slow, enigmatic smiles.

"Sweet Doro. You've always known how to sort the wheat and the chaff."

Her heart thudded with his compliment, but the moment was short because Charlie and Tom approached and stopped in front of the confidante, their faces puffed with embarrassment turned sullen and angry. They resembled two ten-year-olds who had just lost a scuffle. Charlie frowned down at his guardian.

"If this is society, I don't think much of it. I'd as soon go back to Devon until Amelia's ball."

"N-no, don't d-do that," Tom stuttered, stricken by the thought of losing his new friend. Dorothea felt for him and, knowing Garreth's thoughts on the matter, she was half-afraid he would agree with his ward. She made a desperate attempt to change the course of the young Marquess's thoughts.

"Well, that would certainly give Miss Kettling a victory. Imagine how powerful it would make her feel to know that one snub from her could drive a gentleman out of society."

"And she w-would think that," Tom said, throwing a look back over his shoulder. "Charlie, you can't l-let her get away with it."

"No, er . . . no." Confusion replaced Charlie's anger. He looked from Dorothea to Garreth, to Tom and then down at the floor. Firm decision set his features.

"I'll talk to Amelia," he said as if that settled the matter.

"But first you'll do the pretty to Lady Jersey," Garreth said, rising.

Dorothea looked up to see Sally approaching. With her was a gentleman whose features were familiar, but she was unable to put a name to the aristocratic but pallid face.

"I declare, Doro, all the women in London will want to know your secret," Lady Jersey said, smiling. "With so many beauties to meet, Lord Ingleforth is desirous only of renewing his acquaintance with you.''

No one could have been more surprised than Doro, who remembered the gentleman after she heard his name, though why he should be so interested in meeting her was a mystery. They had never been truly acquainted. In her first season she had been introduced to him and he had danced one dance with her. As far as she knew, he had never noticed her again. Still, it behooved her to be polite.

"It has been a long time, Lord Ingleforth. Do you still dance as well as ever?"

"I endeavour to please, my lady," he said smoothly as he bowed over her hand. The smile that played around his thin lips did not reach his eyes.

Lady Jersey had done her duty by the lord and Doro, but as one of the hostesses of Almack's, she was responsible for introducing many of the young people to each other. She turned her attention toward Charlie and Tom.

"I am certainly remiss in not introducing you two around," she said, stepping between them and accepting their arms. "With so many lovely ladies about, we cannot have you standing by yourselves. Is there anyone you'd especially like to meet?"

As she asked the question, she looked pointedly in the direction of the Kettling beauty. Dorothea raised her hand in an automatic protest. Garreth, who had been exchanging greetings with Ingleforth, turned to stop her, but it was Charlie who spoke first.

"The young lady in yellow isn't dancing," he said, inclining his head in the opposite side of the room from Miss Kettling. Looking in that direction, Dorothea was surprised to see a rather stout young lady in a primrose muslin with too many flounces. She was in conversation with another young female, much too tall and no better aspected.

"Yes, those two seem to be rather jolly," Tom said, manfully seconding Charlie's choice.

"My heavens." Lady Jersey sounded breathless with surprise. "I can see you two will be the rage of the ton hostesses."

As Sally led the two young men away, Lord Ingleforth bowed to Dorothea again.

"With Lord Tolver's permission I will steal you away for a dance, my lady."

"I wonder if I still remember how," Dorothea mused aloud and allowed him to lead her onto the floor. As she took her place in the set of the country dance, she stood facing the confidante where Garreth sat alone. He returned her smile, but he appeared to be seriously watching the dancers, keeping an eye on her, as well as their charges.

"It's been a long time since I've seen you in London," Lord Ingleforth said, reclaiming her attention.

"Yes, I've been living retired," she said, but couldn't add more since the dance started and they were almost immediately swept apart.

For the past week she had been gratified to find many people remembered her, and as she moved from partner to partner in the dance, several gentlemen spoke to her with the freedom of having been introduced to her years ago. Since she had trouble putting names and faces together, she was gratified that most of them had no trouble recalling her name.

She had not danced for years, and found the steps required most of her concentration. The next time she chanced to see the confidante at the end of the room, it was empty. Garreth had doubtless gone in search of company, she thought, and tried to convince herself not to be too disappointed if he did not come back when the dance was over. She should just be grateful for the interest she'd had from him. She tried to keep her mind on the steps of the dance, but the enjoyment had suddenly evaporated.

BUT SHE WOULD HAVE BEEN surprised indeed to know how much her affairs interested Lord Tolver, and that his leaving the confidante had as much to do with helping to establish Tom in the right circles as Charlie. After the dance had begun he had sauntered around the room until he found Lady Jersey.

When he first approached her she was in the company of Emily Cawper, and they were listening to a portly matron who, judging from Sally's bored expression, was trying to ingratiate herself with the hostesses of Almack's. Garreth leaned against the wall and waited. It wasn't long before Lady Jersey's innate restlessness caused her attention to stray and she noticed him. In less than a minute she had taken advantage of the matron's pause for breath, excused herself and turned to join him.

"Am I remiss?" She opened her fan and fluttered it, her eyes glittering in amusement. "Have I left you on your own when I could have introduced you to some charming antidote?"

Garreth opened his snuffbox and took a small pinch, all the while watching her carefully.

"Would you dare it?"

"Never," she said, laughing. "No doubt you've some scheme in mind. What are you up to, Garreth?"

"Reintroduce me to Clair Arnside."

A shade of confusion tinted her eyes for a moment, but Lady Jersey was as quick of understanding as she was voluble.

Years before either Garreth, Sally or Dorothea had made their entrance into society, Lady Clair, oldest daughter of the Duke of Richfield, had shocked society by marrying John Arnside, the fourth son of an impoverished baron. Though she had been considered to have made the misalliance of the decade, her faith in Arnside was later proven. His grasp of foreign policy had won him an an important government post, and by profitably investing her considerable dowry he was ably providing for five active sons. The young Arnsides were emerging as the leaders of a set of young blades who occasionally cut up larks, but who eschewed the gaming hells in favour of Corinthian activities.

"My apologies, Garreth, but you really take this guardianship seriously."

"No, just seeing to it that the young scamp breaks his neck so I can inherit." He grinned as he watched her mentally run through the Landruth family tree to ascertain whether or not he was serious. She shook her head at him.

THOUGH THE DANCE brought them together frequently, Dorothea was glad she need not keep up a constant conversation with Lord Ingleforth. His height made it difficult for her to see his expression, but she had the distinct impression he was assessing her. His lips kept smiling, but his eyes were speaking a different language, one she felt she should best avoid understanding.

She was doubly relieved to find Lady Harriet seated on the confidante when he led her back to her place. She was also intrigued to find Lady Amelia speaking urgently to her mother, bright spots of colour highlighting her cheeks.

"Careful how you go, my girl," Lady Harriet said.

"Mama!"

"Hush!"

Dorothea cringed when she feared she might be privy to a family contretemps, but as Lady Harriet looked up at the approaching couple, the high-nosed lady's eyes twinkled with mischief.

"Ingleforth!" She spoke the name in an explosion of sound.

"Lady Harriet." He bowed. "It is indeed a pleasure. I believe you are acquainted with my mother."

"Knew her at school. Worst seat and hands in the country." She pointed one imperious finger across the room. "Go get me Glissenton. *His* mother could ride."

Not even Lord Ingleforth's poise could withstand the abruptness of the countess, and he blinked before he regained his composure. His bow was reproving in its perfection before he left the ladies to do her bidding.

He'd no sooner turned his back than Lady Harriet looked up at her daughter, who appeared pleased.

"You mind how you go, my girl."

"I'm just going to give carrot-top something to think about," Lady Amelia replied.

"No leading him on, mind. He's well enough in his way, but he's not your sort, and Charlie's old enough to fight his own battles."

Though the first of their conversation had left Dorothea puzzled, she now understood what was afoot. Lord Ingleforth was approaching the group around Miss Kettling. Lady Harriet saw the direction of her gaze and gave her a smile which transformed the stiff, autocratic features into the face of a mischievous girl.

"Maria Kettling's got her heart set on Glissenton."

"And Lady Amelia—" Dorothea stopped just short of expressing herself. It would not do to accuse the young lady of trying to cut out the beauty in Lord Glissenton's affections, though that was clearly what she had in mind.

"Didn't like the way that Kettling chit cut Charlie," Lady Harriet said. "Can't say I blame her. Never cared for rude people. No excuse for it."

"No," Dorothea said a little breathlessly, but the shocks from the countess's forceful personality had not stopped.

"Oh, should give you a hint which will save you a lot of grief. Leave Ingleforth alone. Shocking gambling debts. He's for the basket unless he can marry the ready."

"Well, I, uh..." Dorothea could conceive of no answer, though in truth she had sensed what Lady Harriet was telling her.

"Too bad you let your coming circumstances be puffed off so soon. Honey draws flies."

"My circum— What . . . who . . . *I* don't even know exactly how I'll be placed." She could hardly believe what she was hearing.

"Someone has made it their business, or at least has spread rumours. Easy over the ground until you find out about anyone whom you choose for your company. Speaking of company, are you taking Farrie to the Masquerade at the Opera House?"

Lady Harriet's abrupt remarks gave Dorothea the feeling that she was standing in the centre of a spinning top, but the last question brought her to a halt. She felt her face stiffen in disapproval. Her immediate reaction was to say certainly not, but the countess was Garreth's friend. Dorothea was also giving consideration to Farrie's feelings about potentially losing her new and only friend in London, and so wondered if she should allow the association if Lady Harriet was so lenient. Not even an earl's daughter could maintain her reputation if she stepped beyond the line.

But then Garreth had told her the Easterlys lived much retired. Perhaps she should give a hint in return.

"I really had not given it any thought," she said cautiously. "Of course, having been out of society for so long, I find I'm not overly familiar with what is acceptable today." The countess's sharp eyes were twinkling again, throwing Doro into more confusion, but she strove to continue. "It could be that my memory fails me and I am thinking of an entirely different place, but during my season it was not thought acceptable."

"Ha! Girl, don't be mealymouthed when you believe something. Just wondered where you stood on things. Ah, here's Glissenton,'' Lady Harriet rose and turned to Lord Glissenton who looked slightly stunned.

"I'm thirsty. Glissenton, you may take Lady Amelia and me into the other room for some refreshments.''

As Lord Glissenton meekly led the two ladies away, Dorothea breathed a sigh of relief. Lady Harriet was the most overpowering female she had ever met, and she wondered if it was an association her nerves could stand. She had often thought herself made of sterner stuff than most well-born females, but even her courage had a limit.

Still, courage might be necessary, she thought. Garreth had not returned. Perhaps he had found more congenial company elsewhere. Her heart could hope, but she had known from the first that she could not compete for his affections.

CHAPTER FIVE

WITH A SUDDEN START, Dorothea realized she had not
seen Farrie since she'd left the dance floor, an unfor-
givable omission in a chaperon, she thought, looking
around. She suffered a moment's near panic before
she caught sight of a white muslin skirt trimmed in
pink and green and just the glimpse of Farrie's dark,
glossy curls as she stood by Tom's side in a circle of
young people.

Where the plump young lady in primrose had stood
with only her friend for company, the number had
grown to half a score, with the preponderance in favour of the young ladies.

Beyond Tom and Farrie she could see Charlie's
bright blond head, and a shift in the circle revealed
Lord Farling, who remained by Farrie's side but was
in some bantering conversation with a tall, spindly
young woman in an atrocious green muslin.

Though she could not see his face, she knew Tom's
stance well enough to tell he was relaxed, as he nodded his head emphatically.

Perhaps all her worries had been for nothing, she
thought, as she looked up to see Garreth and Sally
coming across the room. Her head was raised slightly
as she addressed him with some remark, and his answer must have been a thrust or parry, since Lady

Jersey's eyes widened, she frowned and bit back a laugh.

"Be thankful I didn't foist every antidote in the room on you," Lady Jersey said as they came to stand by the confidante. Sally had crossed the room with Garreth in order to bring Dorothea a message from an aging spinster who had left early.

"And Lady Caroline expects you to call sometime next week," Sally said as she finished the message. "She's really too old to get out much, but she will come to look over the new arrivals."

They were suddenly joined by Charlie, his eyes bright, and after her years with Tom, Dorothea was aware he was big with either news or questions, apparently for Sally, since he was gazing at her with an air of an energetic puppy on a leash. So noticeable was his anxiety that Garreth, Dorothea and Sally turned to him.

"Are you ready for more introductions, Lord Ridgeley?" Sally asked him.

"Thank you, Mr. Nelson has been taking care of that, but we're in a hobble, Lady Jersey. How are we supposed to ask people to dance if they aren't allowed to waltz? There're several on the program." He held out the offending paper as proof.

Since the next number on the program was a waltz, his problem did warrant immediate attention.

"The young ladies will wait until they are given permission," Sally said crisply. She waved her hand to indicate a number taking the floor, among them Miss Kettling. "I would think even as far away as Elmridge you would have known that."

Dorothea had heard of Lady Jersey's famous set-downs, and a cold knot formed in her stomach. Knowing Garreth's fondness for the boy, she did not expect him to take it lightly. His mouth tightened, but before he could speak, Charlie took the matter out of his hands.

Used to his guardian's blunt, casual way of speaking, Charlie's mulish expression showed he had recognized a censure, but he had never received one couched in malice and did not perceive it as such. Unused to viewing himself as a young swell about town, and accustomed to seeing Lord Tolver's other friends as surrogate parents when he was in their company, he accepted the most feared tongue in London society in the same spirit. Like any youngling, secure in his family circle and knowing his grievances will be heard, he retorted in kind.

"Yes, and I dashed might as well go back home if the only ones who win the approval of the patronesses are high-nosed people who can be friendly one day and the next they're rude to a fellow in front of his friends."

"Charlie!" Garreth's voice was soft, slightly amused that he had not knuckled under to the stiff patroness, but the warning was plain. The young marquess blushed.

Dorothea threw a quick look at Sally whose eyes had widened in disbelief, for clearly it had been years since anyone had dared answer one of her setdowns. But being quick of mind, she had understood what had brought about a comment about high-nosed people.

"I beg pardon if I was out of line." Charlie gave his apology grudgingly, without a hint of remorse, though his anger faded and he turned a pair of imploring and hopeful eyes on his guardian's powerful friend. "But it seems hard, Lady Jersey, when I had to take all those lessons, and the only really jolly partners we've found can't waltz."

As Dorothea watched, not daring to interrupt, she saw that her old friend was no more impervious to the young marquess's unaffected charm than she herself would be. With her considerable reputation as a dragon at stake, it wasn't surprising that Lady Jersey tried to keep her face stiff to hide the softening of her emotions.

"I can tell from the noise on that side of the room that if I gave my permission you would turn it into a romp."

Charlie appeared as surprised as if someone had suggested he sweep a chimney. "Of course we wouldn't! We'll be all dignity—on the dance floor." The innocence of his smile almost hid the qualification of his answer, which was tantamount to a boyish threat of blackmail. Not even Dorothea could believe he could escape Sally's wrath a second time.

She wanted to speak up, to deflect the lightning she was sure Sally would throw, but after a slight frown, Lady Jersey shook her head in resignation.

"Garreth, I can tell you had a hand in raising this young scamp. Society may not live through it. Come with me," she said to Charlie. "I'll see what I can do."

All happy enthusiasm again, Lady Jersey led Charlie toward the group of young people.

"It's going to be jolly, because Miss Duval told me they had lesson parties, and they all learned the steps. She's a good sort, full of fun and gig, the best . . ."

As they moved out of hearing, Dorothea reached behind her, fumbling for the arm of the confidante and lowering herself to the seat with as much grace as her weakening knees would allow.

"I wonder if you have anything to worry about," she said to Garreth. "If Charlie can handle Sally, he should have no trouble in society."

"Young fool, I should have sent him to school," Garreth said, sitting beside her.

"I was afraid," she admitted. "I had visions of a long friendship coming to an end at that moment."

"No," he said, his eyes on the group across the room, where by the bright faces and silent attention the young people were giving Lady Jersey, they were receiving the coveted permission, but also being warned against letting their high spirits lead them into the exceptionable.

"I decided to take your advice," Garreth said.

"Mine? I'm not persuaded I gave any." Upon reviewing their recent exchanges, she could not remember having suggested anything of a particular nature.

"You did say we couldn't take their experiences as a repeat of our own," he answered, drumming his fingers softly against the pale straw-coloured silk of the padded seat. When he turned to gaze at her she saw that enigmatic expression in his eyes again, one she had not learned how to read.

"Wise Doro," he said softly. "How often I could have used your sage advice during the past twelve years."

She would have liked to answer, to disclaim that wisdom with which he was crediting her. She was fervently grateful for his good opinion, but her head seemed full of cotton wool, and her recalcitrant tongue was no longer hers to control. She was still looking down at her hands when Garreth gave an irritated grunt, which warned her the mood had been broken.

"There's young Vernon Tinsley dividing his attention between us and that young horde. He's after an introduction to Farrie. I'd have thought Tom would have brought her back by now. I'll go take care of it." He rose, but turned to look down at Doro. "Don't get stolen away. I need to talk to you about a certain matter."

Still a little off-balance by his compliment and insensibly flattered by his desire to continue their conversation, she was not able to prevent a nervous laugh, which came out in an irritating twitter.

"I doubt anyone will spirit me away," she said.

"Then more fool them," he said with a slow smile as he left.

Her emotions in a turmoil, Dorothea watched him nod to a personable-looking young man who joined the viscount as he crossed the room to the group Lady Jersey had just left. By his reception in the group, his reputation as a great gun, Tom's description, had obviously preceded him. After the formality of introducing Mr. Tinsley to Farrie, he asked one of the young ladies to take the floor, and it was a highly gratified young lady who stepped out with him, followed by three of her friends partnered by Tom, Charlie and Lord Farling.

Viscount Tolver's ton was too good to allow him to express even a hint of his feelings for society to see, but as he took his place on the floor, for a brief moment his gaze met Dorothea's, and his fleeting explanation was clear to her. For this dance at least, he would see to it that the young sprigs under their aegis kept their promise to Sally and did not turn it into a romp.

Much to her dismay, Lord Ingleforth came to join her on the confidante before the waltz was over. In the half hour he stayed with her she three times refused his requests that she take the floor with him, on the excuse that she must be available to Farrie when the young lady was ready to be returned to her chaperon. She had been led into one lapse of expected responsibility that evening and she would not risk another.

It was plain that Lord Ingleforth had set himself to be pleasant, and she listened to him as he pointed out various people she vaguely remembered and many she had not previously known. But underlying his carefully chosen remarks, she was aware of his cool, well-thought-out efforts to please. Contrasting him with Garreth's casual remarks, which were so thoughtless at times as to be almost rude with no malice intended, she found the elegant lord singularly colourless.

Though Garreth had asked her for another opportunity to talk with her, he did not return to the sofa as she had expected. Her spirits lowered through the evening as she caught only glimpses of him on the dance floor, usually partnering a female not in the first bloom of youth, but they all shared the similarity of well-grounded social poise and an elegance of dress she could not equal.

The evening was becoming a boring repetition of young men being brought to be introduced to Farrie, for Sally was certainly exerting an effort to see that her friend's ward was not left standing.

But while her pleasure in the evening had ended with Garreth's leaving her side, Tom and Farrie had enjoyed themselves immensely.

"If it weren't for Charlie's embarrassment, I'd be glad that chit snubbed us," Tom said with a yawn as they were riding home in the carriage. "Miss Duval and her sister Sarah are a pair of henwits."

"You danced with both of them twice," Farrie reminded him.

"They're good sorts," Tom allowed sleepily, "and I didn't see you disdaining Mr. Nelson or Lord Farling, but I wouldn't give them marks for more brains than hair, or looks, either."

"I know," Farrie agreed, "but they're nice, and I didn't feel at all like I'd make some stupid mistake."

"Like dumping lemonade on them." Her brother grinned.

"Or causing them to step in a puddle." Farrie laughed.

"Or putting a slice of cake on a chair for someone to sit on." Tom continued with the list as they both laughed, but Dorothea suddenly alert to what they were saying, came bolt upright.

"Nothing like that happened?" she asked, aghast.

"Oh, no, dear Doro, we were models of mannerly behaviour," Farrie said, hugging her fondly. "But during supper we fell into conversation about the things we thought would be the most horrid to have happen."

"Then leading one to step into a puddle was most certainly Lord Tolver's suggestion, or Charlie made it for him," Dorothea said with a soft smile of memory. "He once did that to me when we were attending one of our first grown-up affairs. He was trying to be gallant and was even more embarrassed than I was."

But that had been a Garreth of seventeen, and while the poised gentleman of thirty-five seemed unlikely to cause his companion such distress, she doubted she was likely to find out. The hopes which she had allowed to grow earlier in the evening had been dashed when he did not return as he had promised.

The next afternoon she was sure she had put Garreth out of her mind when she received a letter from him asking her to go out with him in his curricle the next morning.

The Sailings were accustomed to the earlier hours of country life and Dorothea had breakfasted, dressed for her ride and had written several replies to invitations before Garreth was announced shortly before ten.

Well aware no gentleman liked to keep his horses standing, even when the weather was not likely to do them harm, she had beside her escritoire her hat, gloves, a paisley shawl and her reticule and had but to put on her hat while he watched appreciatively.

"I should have known you wouldn't keep me waiting," he said, and led the way outside, not speaking again until he had handed her up into the curricle.

Seeing they were taking a southerly and not westerly direction, Dorothea gave Garreth an enquiring look, which he correctly interpreted as a question as to where they were going.

"We'll ride in Green Park," he said. "I've no patience with being interrupted this morning."

"Should I be terrified that you'll inform me of some vile plot or scheme?" she asked.

"Hardly," he said shortly, his attention at the moment on a pair of dogs chasing a cat which seemed undecided whether to seek shelter by climbing a tree or dashing between the wheels of the curricle. The pair of sleek bays were eyeing the cat and prancing sideways as it ran along the street pursued by the yapping dogs.

It was not until they had turned into the park that Garreth relaxed, brought the horses to a slow walk and was able to turn his attention to the subject of conversation which had been the excuse for the morning ride.

"You couldn't have missed Harry's—Lady Harriet's—attitude the other night," he said without preamble. "She wanted to find out what sort of person you were, and knowing her, she made it uncomfortably obvious."

"I was aware that I was an object of some speculation," she replied, not sure how to phrase what had seemed a blatant examination of her character.

"That's one way of putting it." He chuckled and then turned serious again. "The truth is, Harry finds herself in a fix. She's promised Amelia her season and Lady Cynthia is cutting up stiff."

"Lady Cynthia, the great-aunt who is ill?" Dorothea remembered the conversation she'd had with Garreth several days ago on the subject.

"That's the one. Harry comes across as a Tartar, but she could take lessons from the old lady. It seems Lady Cynthia is insisting her time has come and will accept nothing less than Harry's undivided attention. Harry believes it no more than I, but she can't take the chance that the old woman might not be telling the truth. She raised Harry, and for all her selfish ways, Lady Cynthia was good to her."

"And Lady Harriet's interest in me has something to do with her great-aunt?"

"Smart Doro. I like a woman who is quick-minded." Garreth gave her a swift and boyish smile which twisted her heart.

"Not to make three volumes of it, she would like for you to move into Wilton House, to be there with Lady Amelia."

Dorothea stared at him, aghast at the suggestion. He looked down at her, frowned and shook his head.

"I think I've made a mull of it, so hear me through. You know they've a ball in the planning stages, the invitations are already out, so it's impossible for Harry to close the house."

"But Lady Harriet must have *some* female relative and it would be far better . . ." She paused as Garreth emphatically shook his head.

"Won't do. She may be able to scare up some distant relatives, but they're guaranteed to be stuffy and stiff. Harry's always given Amelia credit for having good sense and let her choose her own course—within bounds. A starched-up old stiff is just the sort to put so many restrictions on her that she'd kick over the traces."

"But if her own relatives can't handle Lady Amelia I certainly can't."

"You won't need to. You treat her just like you do Farrie and she'll be fine. Amelia knows what's expected of her, and she'll behave unless she's driven into rebellion, which is what that kin of Harry's would do."

"What made her think of me?" Dorothea was still half-stunned by the suggestion.

"I did." He gave her another grin. "Tom and Farrie prove you'd be the right sort for Amelia and—" he paused, gave her a frank look "—I thought it might lighten your financial load."

Dorothea reminded herself this was Garreth, her old playmate, her friend, and the man to whom she had given her heart years ago. Perhaps the latter was the reason her pride rose so suddenly.

"I'm not a pauper, Garreth." She fumbled with the ribbons of her reticule to keep from looking at him.

"No, but you've had to live like one," he said with a savagery which brought her gaze up fleetingly to his. "Don't tell me you're not having to make some shifts, and think how much easier it would be if instead of bearing the cost of Lindsterhope House, you could let it for the rest of the season. Think of how much more you could do for Farrie and Tom."

The picture of a white muslin gown trimmed in silver lace came back to her mind. She had seen it in the shop of Madame Fransais, one of the most fashionable modistes on Bond Street, and knew that Farrie would be a vision in it, but it had been out of the reach of her purse. She had sighed and let the dream go, but if she consented to what seemed to her to be an outrageous scheme Farrie might still have it.

"Farrie and Amelia are friends already," Garreth went on. "Tom would like it, I know. He and Charlie will be back and forth across the garden at all hours, but it will be more convenient when they want to ride. Both stables are full of mounts. We'll send the pack of them to work off their energies in the park every morning. It'll give us a break, don't you think?''

Dorothea was becoming confused again. ''Both stables? The garden? Forgive me if I sound like a parrot, but I don't understand.''

Garreth grinned. ''We're right next door. Good thing, or I'd have had to rent out Tolver House and hire another one. And I don't think we've straightened out whose cattle is whose since those two brats learned to ride.''

Dorothea tried to still her swirling thoughts. The financial relief would in itself be a blessing. The two young ladies would be happy about it, she knew, and Tom would be no less pleased. That morning he had ridden out with Charlie and two of the five young Arnside gentlemen, a bit put down because he was forced to accept the loan of a hack from Charlie, but pleased that his mount was well bred and drew the admiration of passersby.

If Wilton House was indeed next door to Tolver House, then she would doubtless see more of Garreth than ever. Would that be a point in her favour or against? She was beginning to count too heavily on his company, though she knew her wayward hopes could be leading her toward disappointment.

''There's just one thing that bothers Harry,'' Garreth said. His voice had changed tone, grown slightly hoarser, as if he were struggling to bring up an unwelcome issue.

"Pray tell me what it is, so the bubble can burst before I start spending the money I saw myself saving," she said, trying to keep her voice light.

"It's Ingleforth. Harry doesn't like him, and she doesn't want him around Amelia. She wants to be certain you're not entertaining any plans in that direction before we come to an agreement."

Dorothea laughed aloud. "I'm persuaded our sympathies are in complete agreement on that head. I know nothing about the man, save that his efforts to be pleasant leave me thinking of something else entirely."

"He showed you a marked amount of attention," Garreth said, speaking each word with a preciseness which, from long experience with his moods, warned Dorothea he disliked the subject but was determined to pursue it. She found herself inordinately pleased that he had noticed the time Lord Ingleforth spent in her company.

"The decision was his," she said with a laugh, "and since he in no way offended me, I could not in good conscience send him about his business." But Garreth's aloof expression warned her she needed to say more. "I'm aware Lady Harriet thinks he's after my fortune, though how he can know anything of it surpasses my comprehension."

"Your expectations are rather better known than you might wish," he said. "Someone has made it their business to spread the particulars."

The story put about by some unknown person was indeed circulating if Garreth had also heard it. Dorothea could not imagine where it'd come from, but the implied result was obvious.

"Then both you and Lady Harriet expect me to be beset with fortune-hunters?" she asked lightly. "Shall I distrust and enquire into the gambling habits of every gentleman who shows me any attention?"

She had meant her remark to be bantering, but Garreth had not taken it in that spirit. His silence seemed self-explanatory.

"You do," she said quietly.

"How can I say what their intentions are?" he remarked shortly and suddenly became busy with the reins. "That would be maladroit of me."

"Oh?"

"It's not my place or aim to give credibility to any suitor who approaches you, but I'd think you'd take it as an insult if I said your fortune was the only reason for their attention."

"But that's what you believe," she pursued, her spirits lowering again.

"How could I think that?" He dropped his hands, giving his cattle the office to move at a brisker pace. "I don't remember that you had a fortune coming when I wrote that letter sixteen years ago."

His sudden reference to his awkward, boyish offer gave her pause, and she fingered the ribbons on her reticule as she sought some way to answer.

"Ah, but I'm persuaded that you didn't understand the value of a fortune then," she said. "And while your willingness to assist a friend in difficulties was heroic, you know you were much relieved that I did not respond."

"I find it truly amazing that you know me so well you can make my decisions for me," he said, and flicked the reins, putting the horses to a fast trot.

CHAPTER SIX

DESPITE GARRETH'S ASSURANCES that she would find Wilton House a residence in which not a jot of effort would be spared to see to her comfort, Dorothea could not feel easy about the arrangement, and when he returned her to Green Street, she had agreed only to chaperon Amelia to Lady Sefton's ball that night, and at that time she would give him a definite answer.

Indeed she felt for Lady Harriet's predicament, and would have been delighted to have Amelia come and stay with her. She could also understand that, with preparations under way for a ball and the invitations already sent, Wilton House must remain open, but for her to move not only herself, but Tom, Farrie and such servants as she decided not to send back to Marvale did seem a bit excessive. And what if Lady Cynthia took a sudden turn of good health, and after Dorothea had let her house, Lady Harriet was able to return and had no more need for her?

Such thoughts were occupying her mind when she entered the drawing room to find Tom and Farrie in earnest conversation. They had not heard the opening of the door and she was privileged to see them sitting together, each holding a teacup and saucer, their attention on a subject which made Tom voluble and

Farrie nod her dark head when she was not adding a comment of her own.

Dorothea paused to watch them for a moment before crossing the room. Tom glanced up and saw her. He rose immediately, a wide smile lighting his face.

"There, you've caught us with our nefarious secret," he said, and his manner of speaking was an inadequate cover for hiding the subject which had been under discussion.

"We are found out," Farrie added breathlessly. "You must surely discover that every time you leave us alone we become very idle and expensive with a forbidden pot of tea."

"You do not include me in your luxurious interludes?" Dorothea asked. "I must be broken-hearted."

It would have been thought wonderful indeed if any of the three had succeeded in fooling the others. They were not by nature dissemblers, and had had too little practice to overcome any defect in that direction.

"I will remove my hat," Dorothea said, "Farrie shall pour me a cup of that tea, and Tom, you shall tell me the secret you were sharing with your sister when I came in."

"It cannot be a secret, since you have returned from your ride with Lord Tolver," Farrie said as she poured the tea. "I have had a note from Amelia about what her mama and uncle—Lord Tolver—have planned. Tom and Charlie quite have it that we will be moving into Wilton House today."

"Well, I do think it would be fun to be all together," Tom said. "Charlie says we will all ride in the park in the mornings. You and Farrie will have the use of the Wilton carriages to shop and ride in the park.''

Farrie had at first been nodding her head in enthusiastic approval of Tom's list of advantages, but suddenly her face clouded in doubt. Her brother had been watching her.

"Farrie, don't tell me you have suddenly turned disapproving."

"It occurs to me that the advantages are all for us and none for Doro," she said slowly. "We have not considered that Wilton House would be much larger, and there is Amelia's ball to think of. All the management would fall on Dorothea if Lady Harriet cannot return."

"Oh, there's nothing to that," Tom said with what at first sounded like a sublime male disregard for the chores of running a household.

"Men do not understand a woman's tasks," Dorothea said soothingly when Farrie appeared to take offence for her sake, but Tom had not been belittling the female role.

"Charlie has said there will be nothing for Doro to do," he objected. "According to Charlie, Lady Harriet has not the least interest in running her household, and so has a dragon of a housekeeper who manages everything."

"Then it will be perfect for Doro, too," Farrie said, sitting back and giving a satisfied sigh.

Dorothea sipped her tea, thinking she might as well give in. Though she could not like it that Farrie and Tom had been enlisted by their friends to encourage the move, she knew she was being unfair. Lady Amelia was doubtless acting out of a desire to remain in town, and while her aims might be slightly selfish, it was not in the nature of young people to consider mundane practicalities.

Charlie and Tom were forming a close friendship, and no doubt the marquess had spoken of the advantages of their living side by side with his usual enthusiasm, which swayed Tom, who so wanted a friend.

"Until I've spoken with Lady Harriet, I won't make a decision," Dorothea said, hoping to forestall a final decision until she'd had the leisure to consider it more carefully.

"But you cannot," Farrie said looking suddenly worried. "She is already on her way back to Salvermain." As proof, Farrie opened her reticule and extracted two sheets of heavy, folded paper, and handed them to Dorothea. Glancing over them she saw the large, round letters of an immature fist, and reading the part Farrie pointed out, she discovered Lady Harriet had ordered rooms prepared for the Sailings, and even such servant accommodation as would be required to house whatever personal staff Dorothea considered necessary.

> ...for Uncle Garreth assured Mama that you would come, and Papa only stops in town long enough for you, Tom and Lady Lindsterhope to come to us. Then he will be away also.

"I can't believe Garreth committed me before he even mentioned the matter," she said, looking up from the letter.

"But you would not say no, and leave him to look nohow with his friends," Tom said with an assurance he had no right to display.

Yet strangely enough, his statement acted most powerfully on Dorothea. Sixteen years before he had been willing to rescue her from her troubles, even going so far as to make her an offer of marriage. Now he had given his word to Lady Harriet with the full expectation that she would return the favour by assisting him to rescue his friends. It would be beyond anything if she were to let him down.

"Then I suppose there is no help for it," she said with resignation. "I must compose a note to Lord Wilton, since his wife is out of town—" She gave a start and sloshed tea into the saucer as a thud sounded in the hall.

"What was that?" she asked, putting the cup and saucer down and rising to see what was amiss.

"Oh, someone just dropped something." Farrie tried to sound nonchalant, but her face coloured.

"Something?" Dorothea asked, suddenly suspicious.

"Sounded a b-bit like a trunk," Tom replied, suddenly busy with the folds of his neckcloth.

Dorothea turned, her eyes snapping with an anger she had not felt in years, not since she'd discovered the concealed letters from Garreth and Sally. Once again she felt used and conspired against.

"I was away from this house just above an hour, and in my absence—"

"Oh, Doro, d-don't be angry," Tom said, dropping his nonchalant approach and hurriedly crossing the space between them. "We th-thought it would be what you would w-wish."

"We only wanted to surprise you," Farrie said, putting her sewing aside and standing, unshed tears bringing a sparkle to her eyes. "Amelia sent her personal maid—"

"And Charlie sent his own valet, knowing I d-didn't have one."

"We were going to spare you all the trouble of directing the packing," Farrie explained.

"We didn't know you hadn't quite made up your m-mind."

In the midst of their explanations the door to the drawing room was suddenly thrown open to reveal a harassed footman, who was imperiously ordered out of the way by Lord Tolver in a voice which could have thundered across a cavalry regiment.

"Get in there, you two!"

Lady Amelia and the Marquess of Ridgeley made their entrance in a far different mood from their first visit. They were both pale and chastened. Behind Lady Amelia a plainly dressed maid followed to the doorway, thought better of entering and backed out of sight.

Lord Tolver strode in behind them, his face dark with anger. Before Dorothea could utter a word, he jerked off his hat and pointed it in the direction of the young lord and lady who had preceded him.

"Doro, I knew nothing about this," he disclaimed. "If you want to thrash the lot of them for cramming your fences, I'll hold them for you."

"But we didn't do anything wrong," Charlie said, not much daunted by the threat. "All we were doing was helping out Lady Lindsterhope."

"That's all," Amelia seconded. "We just wanted to save her the effort of packing."

"And it didn't occur to any of you to give her time to make a decision before you shipped her off to Curzon Street, bag and baggage?" Garreth demanded.

"But of course she wants to come," Charlie said. "Why shouldn't she?"

"Oh, she does." Tom had spoken up, adding Dorothea's only expressed reservation that she had not spoken with Lady Harriet about it.

That brought a spate of explanations from Amelia and Charlie, repeating, adding to and expounding upon the information written in Amelia's note to the effect that her mother had left town at dawn that morning and would be awaiting word that the Sailings were established in Curzon Street. Garreth ordered them to silence. "Now let's approach this matter as straightforwardly as we can under the present circumstances." His frown, which included the Sailings as well as Lady Amelia and Charlie, warned them to be quiet.

"Doro, if you consign us all to the Devil, I don't blame you. But is Tom right? Have you decided to make the move?"

Dorothea possessed a pleasant nature that seldom led her to anger, but she did not lack for spirit, and she was not one to allow herself to be coerced. She hesitated, tempted to put a stop to all the pressure by refusing to set one foot outside the house on Green Street. But while exerting her right to her own decisions would have been a balm to her pride, she would have severely disappointed all four young people, and perhaps put an end to most of the season's activities for Lady Amelia.

"I will be glad to be of service to Lady Harriet," she said, holding on to the shreds of her dignity as Tom and Farrie both tried to embrace her before she had finished her sentence.

"The decision about when you make the move should also be yours," Garreth said, frowning again on the youngsters.

His remark would have carried more effect if over his shoulder she had not at that moment seen two strange servants coming down the stairs carrying another trunk.

"Really?" she said, her voice breathless as one of the men stumbled and righted himself just in time to prevent a disaster. "Then I suppose I must have made it, because I seem to be in the process now."

Garreth turned to see what had caught her attention and watched until the trunk had been set against the far wall of the hall. Then he turned to the four young people.

"Very well," he declared. "You started this move, so suppose you finish getting the clothing packed, over to Wilton House and unpacked in good time for luncheon, if you want any. Doro, I'd much appreciate it if you would offer me a cup of that tea."

"If we're to sit idle and relax, then I believe we should have a fresh pot," she said, walking over to the bellpull while he took a seat on the confidante.

Amelia, Farrie, Tom and Charlie edged toward the doorway and grouped in the hall, occasionally looking back as if expecting Garreth to rescind his edict, or Dorothea to amend it. After several minutes with no reprieve forthcoming, their voices rose in another argument.

"That's just like you, bossing everyone around," Charlie complained. "Why am I the one to go get the carts? Much you know about packing, anyway."

"More than you."

"That's a fine story."

"Well, then tell me, how do *you* fold a net overskirt or protect a pair of silk stockings?"

"Amelia, you have no delicacy of thought at all," Charlie announced. "And if you're going to be that way about it, I *will* go find the carts, and Tom can come with me."

"That's enough of their chatter," Garreth said, getting up and crossing the room. He quietly but firmly closed the door and returned to the confidante, stretching out his long legs.

"Peace and quiet," he said in the manner of a hungry man who has been presented with a succulent dish.

"Thank God for a little peace and quiet." He closed his eyes with a sigh.

While she waited for one of the harassed servants to answer the bell, Dorothea considered the way he was taking his ease. He behaved in a manner more reminiscent of a man in his private quarters than one visiting a lady's drawing room.

His careless assumption that she would accept his present lack of conversation and expected none of the amenities a given well-mannered visitor no longer flattered her. She found it, in fact, extremely irritating.

Clearly she lacked makings of a fictional heroine who could forgive all sights and never think of them again. While she had suppressed her recent anger, realizing that the young people had acted out of enthusiasm and a misguided idea that she would be pleasantly surprised, those feelings had upbraided her nerves, and strong emotions were just under the surface.

Part of the problem, she decided, was Garreth's assumption that she would automatically fall in with his every wish as she had when they were younger and she had been his adoring follower. But he had been so sure she would accede to his wishes that he had promised Lady Harriet success before he had even spoken to her.

Her face felt hot as she recalled her pleasure at his first curt note, then his assumption that she must necessarily prefer the astringent company of his friend to the more pleasant company of the other patrons of Almack's. Obviously she must make a stand, or he would continue to take her for granted as long as she was of the least use to him.

Suddenly Garreth opened his eyes and sat up straight, looking around. "What, no one's answered the bell yet? Are all the servants being chased around by those young devils?"

In her present mood, Dorothea considered suggesting that if the running of her house did not suit him, he might prefer to take his tea at Tolver House, but before she could utter a word he had risen and was striding toward the door, gone through it and disappeared.

Now he was attempting to run her house as though it were his own! She had risen from the chair and had started toward the door when an echo of her own thoughts came back to her.

Silly Doro! You've let all this flurry unsettle your mind, she told herself. Could she be thinking these things of Garreth? Could she actually have been ready to rip up at him because he wanted a cup of tea?

Before she could decide whether she had been in danger of entirely oversetting a generally calm outlook on life, on which she modestly prided herself, or whether she was suddenly quailing from the recognition of something that needed being done, Garreth strode back in the room, looked around, picked up her hat from the table where she had placed it and handed it to her.

"Your cook is threatening to give notice," he said. "At the sight of me in the kitchen, a scullery maid dropped a pan of dishwater in the middle of the floor and is having hysterics. Amelia and Farrie are chasing the footmen and maids about until there's not one available."

"Oh, dear," Dorothea said, not sure she could cope with all the confusion.

"The only normality in the place is that Amelia and Charlie are at it again, hammer and tongs, and you don't want to hear that. We'll take our luncheon at Grillions."

"But I can't leave," she said, ignoring the hat he held out to her as she started toward the door.

"Yes, you can," he said, grabbing his curly-brimmed beaver, which he crammed onto his head without the least regard for his carefully pomaded à la

Brutus. Then he caught up with her, took her by the arm as she stepped out into the hall and bore her inexorably toward the front door.

Caught unexpectedly, she had allowed herself to be propelled through the open door and in full view of any passersby on the street before she could summon her disordered wits and stop him. Disdaining to struggle in public, she nevertheless addressed him in an icy tone.

"Sir, you are far too high-handed, and I desire you let me go right now!"

"That's the last thing you want," he said imperturbably as he led her down the steps and towards his carriage. "It's by my folly you find yourself in this mess, and by abducting you for luncheon I remove you from the consequences without leaving you any cause for shame at your desertion. Now step up into this carriage and put on your hat."

As his authoritative explanation had left her without an answer, there was little she could do but follow his demands. Two young blades on the strut, a jarvey and a baker's delivery boy, were treated to the spectacle of Dorothea hastily tieing the ribbons of her hat. Before she had donned her gloves and slipped her shawl around her shoulders, Garreth had entered the carriage, given the coachman his orders, and they were moving off down the street.

If she had needed more evidence of Garreth's overriding attitude, he had certainly provided it, though how she was to complain of it she could not conceive, since she had earnestly desired to escape the furor brought on by the enthusiasm of the youngsters. Still, she could not meekly accept it without some complaints.

"I have no idea in what case my dresses will be when they reach Wilton House," she complained. "Doubtless I will find my handkerchiefs hidden in my riding boots, and my jewellery among the household linens."

Garreth was at that moment tipping his hat to Lady Fishthorne and her daughter, who were strolling down the street, so he was a moment answering. When he did he gave a thoughtful nod.

"I can see I might have erred in taking you away," he said slowly. "Doubtless Farrie has no turn for conducting a household, though she *is* the same age as Amelia, isn't she?"

Dorothea threw him a darkling look. His implication had been that, at eighteen, many young ladies were married and mistresses of their own households.

"Farrie is knowledgeable in all aspects of running a country house, and can certainly manage in the city," she said stiffly.

Garreth's eyes twinkled. "Ah, so it is your maid that concerns you. Doubtless you had little choice in whom you employed, living as secluded as you did."

"Myra is exceptional and very responsible.... Ah, you are teasing me, though you are entirely correct. Farrie should be able to take command, and Myra and Susanne know how to manage the packing."

"Then why should you worry? Amelia's received a thorough grounding in managing a household from the Mrs. Hicks, the housekeeper, so that only leaves Charlie and Tom to find the carters," he said. "You will have to choose which servants remain in town, but that decision can wait until you've time to think about it. In the meantime give a nod to Princess Esterhazy, who just acknowledged us.''

Dorothea did as he suggested, wondering crossly if she would ever be able to make her own decisions. Then, on rapid reflection, she saw the petulance behind the thought. Obviously she had needed the hint, since she had not noticed one of the patronesses of Almack's. The events of the day had left her with too many thoughts tumbling through her mind to be fully cognizant of everything around her.

Luncheon at Grillions was all she could have asked. A first course of duckling and fresh asparagus, removed with a saddle of veal, and followed by a blackberry compote, all served in elegant surroundings, was the culmination of many of her pleasant imaginings during the bleak years at Marvale.

Nor could she fault Garreth's attention to her every comfort. In private he might be casual of the elegancies of courtesy, but he knew and exercised the exact degree of solicitousness in seeing to it that she was placed so her eyes were shaded from the light of the high windows, that her wineglass was filled, and that their topics of conversation were all pleasant.

Though not since the first of his salad days had he aspired to the dandy set, he was easily the most elegant gentleman in the room. Dorothea was aware that many of the other female diners turned envious eyes toward their table, and indeed, the Marquise de Vilimere, present with Lord Nelewin, her cicisbeo for more than twenty years, seemed so affected by Lord Tolver's close attention to Dorothea's desires, that the

French marquise appeared to become quite cross with her escort's failings.

It occurred to Dorothea that she might be the recipient of the attentions of a man with much wider experience with the ladies than she had ever expected Garreth to possess. The thought bothered her slightly, and she reasoned there would have to have been some women in his life. But more likely, she decided, he was exerting himself to be charming in order to overweigh any lingering doubts she might have about moving to Curzon Street.

As he leaned forward to fill her wineglass again she gazed into his eyes, so filled with a gentle humour she sighed, half-convinced that that one look was worth more than all the advantages she would derive from the move, and even without them, it compensated for all the disadvantages she might find.

CHAPTER SEVEN

LUNCHEON HAD TAKEN Dorothea back into all her girlhood dreams, and had been an interlude she could hardly believe. All too soon it was over, and the sixteen years between her blissful imaginings and the reality of the present dropped away as they entered the carriage.

As if to remind her that life was not always beautiful, the sunny morning had turned into a dreary afternoon and a drizzle filled the air, at first too fine to even seem to fall, but soon it quickened into a light rain.

Since the decision had been made to acquiesce to the plan of moving to Curzon Street they were on the way there to inform Lord Wilton, but when the carriage drew up in front of the house, news of Dorothea's willingness had preceded them in the form of two carts, one full of trunks and the other containing furniture, part of which the Sailings had thought necessary to bring with them from Marvale.

Tom's shaving stand, an indispensable part of his life—though he still lacked a full beard—was precariously balanced on the very back. Entirely too close to the front and the heels of a restive young draft horse, Dorothea saw her favourite sewing table.

"Whatever must Lord Wilton think of such a turn-out on the street in front of his house," Dorothea said, and in her consternation would have reached for the handle of the door and stepped out immediately had Garreth not forestalled her.

"I may have to admit my mistake in leaving it to the halflings," he said, "but falling on your face in the street will not mend matters, old girl."

Dorothea waited for him to open the door and step out. He had no more than reached the pavement when a large portly man with a florid face came smartly down the steps of the house brandishing an open umbrella.

"And here's Wilton's man to protect you from the rain," Garreth said, giving what Dorothea thought to be a singularly unnecessary explanation. "Are you too put out to do the pretty to Lady Lindsterhope?" he asked.

"Don't be daft," snapped the man. "I've not had a chance to speak to the lady yet, and as for being put out, so would you be with that old harridan kicking up her heels and causing such a to-do." He glared at Garreth, and Dorothea thought she had never met such an impudent servant until he bowed to her, a feat in graciousness since he was at the same time holding the umbrella over her.

"Can't tell you how grateful we are, Lady Lindsterhope. For to have Harry called away, and my needing to support her all for that old woman's jealous starts, is dashed unfair to our girl."

"Lord Wilton," Dorothea said, thinking it was highly unusual for the master of the house to come out personally with an umbrella. She had not at first understood Garreth's remark to be a comment on Lord Wilton's odd behaviour.

No less strange was the sudden eruption from the house of nearly a dozen men, hurrying toward the carts. Among them she recognized Paul and Anthony, her two footmen. They swarmed over both carts, hurriedly picking up trunks and untying furniture.

"I must apologize for that," she said, her cheeks heating in embarrassment as she nodded in the direction of the offending pile. "I cannot conceive of what Farrie and Tom could have been thinking of. I will order it returned to Green Street immediately."

"More likely one of Amelia's starts," he said, eyeing the cart critically. "But I wouldn't advise just giving orders willy-nilly. Half of it is in the entrance hall already. Lord, never seen such a mess."

Dorothea felt ready to sink, though Lord Wilton had sounded perfectly complacent about the disruption of his entranceway. It was not until they had ascended the stairs that the full impact of his statement struck her.

The entrance hall of Wilton House had been designed with gracious proportions, and even in its present condition of disarray, it was clear by the freshness of the paint and the stylish wallpaper that no expense had been spared to refurbish it in the latest mode, but what its furnishings might be she had no idea.

In an effort to unload the uncovered carts before the rain damaged the contents, numerous trunks, portmanteaux, hat boxes, chairs, tables, two sofas, a large and particularly hideous buffet had been carried into the house. On the buffet were two dining-room chairs, and straddling them in a precarious position was one of the servant's trunks. Enthroned on that piece of luggage was a large silver epergne, which had been an heirloom of the Sailings family for generations.

Much of the clutter was not the few items which Dorothea had thought wise to bring from Marvale, but the furnishings of Lindsterhope House which had been rescued from the lumber rooms and should have been consigned there again when they closed the house.

Footmen, grooms and one small wizened fellow Dorothea characterized as a tiger were running about calling out orders to each other, all of which were blatantly ignored. Two maids were dashing about taking ineffectual swipes at the moisture on the furnishings as if they were doing a sketchy job of dusting. Halfway up the stairs a stout woman with a consequence double her considerable weight was watching the invasion of the entrance hall with combined astonishment and resignation.

Lord Wilton took no notice of the clutter, beyond frowning down at the maid who was on her knees fiercely determined to wipe up every damp footprint. She was not so lost to her work that she was unaware of the rapidly moving men, and in trying to avoid them she was scuttling around like a distraught beetle.

"Mary, get out of the way," the earl demanded, and as if he expected to be ignored, he stepped over her feet and moved down the narrow passage which had been left between the clutter. Dorothea was to see he had been right not to wait for the maid to move, for beyond muttering unintelligibly under her breath, she continued her useless work.

At the foot of the stairway stood Farrie and Tom, backed against the wall watching the activity as if not sure whether to be entertained or terrified. Clearly the situation had gone beyond their ability to control it.

To add to the confusion, Lady Amelia appeared in the doorway behind them and called out orders to the already harassed servants.

When the arrival of more hurrying footmen with trunks caused Mary, the determined floor scrubber, to back beneath the shelter of a large table, Dorothea took the opportunity to pass her and went to join Farrie and Tom.

Lord Wilton had by that time ascended the steps halfway to speak with a man who, by his clothing, was a gentleman's gentleman and had been standing as if his dignity divorced him from the activity in the hall, though it did not prevent him from being an interested spectator.

The discussion over, the valet had retreated up the steps, and the earl came back down, waving his daughter over to the foot of the stair.

"Listen to me, puss, you're not to give Lady Lindsterhope any cause for worry," he said to her, then to Garreth, he said, "Any of her shenanigans—and see to it that the baroness isn't troubled—you take a riding crop to the girl. With that brat of yours, you probably know the way of it."

Dorothea was shocked to hear the earl address his daughter and Garreth so bluntly in front of the servants, as well as their visitors. Lady Amelia and

Charlie watched him with a frank amiability that showed not the least sign of embarrassment.

"Don't let her starts worry you," he said to Dorothea. "She can keep her seat over rough ground, always brings herself out of her stumbles. Now, if you're settled in, I'll be getting on the road. No telling what's going on at Salvermain."

"I do hope you find the situation in a better case than we fear, and I'm sure Amelia will be as good as gold," Dorothea said with a confidence she did not feel.

"If that's so, I'll come back to see the miracle," Lord Wilton said, and mounted the steps.

His last remark did not augur well for her peace of mind, and glancing around, she wondered, if the present conditions prevailing in Wilton House were what the earl considered settled, what his idea of rough ground could be.

Tom interrupted her thoughts, nervous enough to bring back his stutter.

"Doro, really we c-couldn't help it. All at once the house was full of people Charlie and Amelia brought. They were all moving things. By the time I stopped them from taking the dining-room table, all the furniture from the drawing room was on the c-cart."

Before Dorothea could answer, Charlie had stepped over the floor scrubber with the aplomb of one used to the vagaries of Wilton House and strode across the floor, looking on the clutter with interested eyes.

"I say, Lady Lindsterhope, I think we've overdone it a bit."

"One might get that idea," Dorothea said, knowing that if she gave her feelings free rein, she might succumb to hysterics.

"Oh, well, you can straighten it all out," he said with the insouciance of having given it his all and fate would take care of the rest.

It could not be considered wonderful if she did succumb to hysterics, Doro thought, but made of sterner character, she took a deep breath and turned to face the clutter.

"You'll straighten this mess out," Garreth was saying to Charlie and Tom, but Dorothea rounded on him, striving to keep her voice even.

"No, they will not." Her reply was icy. "It's enough to find half our furnishings here. You will leave it to me before half of Wilton House is taken to Green Street.

"Oh, I don't mind assisting..." Charlie began, but Dorothea turned a quelling look on him.

"I think I have had a sufficiency of assistance from all quarters, so it would please me if I were left to sort this hubble bubble in my own fashion." By the time she had finished this statement her voice had turned glacial, so it was not surprising that after giving a mock shiver, Garreth caught Charlie by the arm and made a hasty retreat out the front door.

After one wide-eyed look, Amelia caught Farrie's hand and started toward the stairs.

"D-Doro..." Tom started, but Amelia reached out and grabbed his coat sleeve, pulling him along.

At the foot of the steps, Dorothea waited until they had reached the landing halfway between the ground and first floors before calling to Mrs. Hicks to ask if she would join her in the hall.

Dorothea had not managed a household for years without knowing the pride which higher servants took in their positions and the ordering of their underlings, so she resolved to tread lightly with the stout woman who ruled Wilton House. While she did reserve a measure of authority, she apologized for oversetting the routine, but she was surprised by the view taken by Mrs. Hicks.

"I doubt there's another pair that can create such a to-do as our young lord and lady," she said with obvious pride. "Not that they didn't mean it for the best, of course, but then that's them all over."

"I'm profoundly thankful you are so understanding," Dorothea said. "Now you obviously know your own people and Lord Tolver's better than I do, so I would appreciate your advice in clearing up this matter."

Nothing, it seemed, could have been more to the taste of the housekeeper than taking the matter in hand. In short order they had identified Dorothea's, Farrie's and Tom's trunks and had them carried up to their rooms along with such small items of furniture as the sewing table and Tom's shaving stand.

The servants owned the remaining trunks, and Dorothea knew most of them would be only too glad to return to Marvale. They had looked upon the visit to London as a high treat, but once there they had found the city to be a noisy, confusing place. After having two parcels stolen by what she had described as an ill-dressed villain with murder in his eye, Mrs. Marks, the Sailing's housekeeper, had confided to her mistress that neither she nor the cook would take on the shopping unless accompanied by one of the footmen. When Bessie and Agnes, respectively the upstairs and parlour maids, took their afternoon and were accosted by a gentleman in his cups, they refused to leave Green Street without escort.

Myra and Susanne, Dorothea's and Farrie's personal maids, would remain, as would Anthony, who, partially instructed by Mrs. Marks, had shown a talent for keeping Tom's clothing in order and acted as the young baron's gentleman.

Three servants were enough to add to the Easterly household, Dorothea thought, and was just giving the instructions for the rest of the luggage to be taken back to Green Street when she chanced to glance toward the door and saw Paul, the second footman, watching her with such a hopeful eye she could not help but understand.

"And Paul will remain, so our errands will not put a burden on your staff," she told Mrs. Hicks. As she watched the young footman's eyes light up, she wondered if the ability to bring that sort of happiness was not a wealth in itself, and so was far more complacent as she assisted the Easterlys' housekeeper in directing the removal of the unwanted furnishings.

When she had received Paul's energetic assurances that he would, with Mrs. Mark's assistance, see the furniture back in place in Lindsterhope House, Mrs. Hicks bustled Dorothea off to the drawing room, promising a refreshing pot of tea, overriding all her guest's objections.

"And you'll not be worrying that this to-do has overset our schedule, not with what we're used to," the housekeeper said, eyeing the stacked furniture as if it were some challenge she looked forward to meeting.

"Still, you cannot like it..." Dorothea started a statement meant to add more pacification, but found herself interrupted.

"When you've had a governess swooning because a pony was in the schoolroom eating her best straw bonnet—that schoolroom on the third floor of Salvermain, mind you—you don't worry over a bit of runaway furniture." Seeing the astonishment and near panic on Dorothea's face, Mrs. Hicks kindly added, "Don't concern yourself that our young lady still brings her horses into the house. She's outgrown all that, but we've had our times."

Across the hall, Jenkins, the silver-haired butler, nodded to Mrs. Hicks, and they both seemed to mentally slip away, doubtless reliving some adventurous episode which would only give Dorothea cause for more worry. She ascended the steps, finding her own way into the large and opulent drawing room of Wilton House.

Clearly the furnishings had not been chosen by a person of timid nature. There was a ferociousness about them which was not at all peaceful. The Egyptian influence then in fashion was predominant in the several sets of tub chairs. Their low mahogany arms terminated in gilded snarling lion masks, which appeared to threaten anyone approaching them with the amiable intention of relaxation. The gilded lion's feet were a match to a huge, ancient Italian coffer which stood against one wall. Despite its carving of a coat of arms, with its depiction of dogs, and bulls all carved in high relief, its shape so suggested a coffin that Dorothea shivered. She resolved to let her bonnet set askew rather than use the ornately etched mirror that hung above the chest in a Precht frame.

Far more interesting to her was another antique, incongruous amid the Egyptian furnishings. An ornate Spanish escritoire, its dark wood trimmed with gilding and brilliant colours, was definitely in the Moorish style. Its twelve small drawers cried out to be opened, explored and used for handy storage of writing supplies. Dorothea thought it would be a pleasure to sit there writing her letters—provided there was no need to send dreadful admissions to Lady Harriet. She could not forget Lord Wilton's look of disbelief when she had assured him Lady Amelia would be well behaved.

Behind her the door opened and a maid entered, bringing a tea tray. Dorothea had just removed her bonnet and the maid had just set down the tray on a marquetry table when Amelia came in. Breathless as if she had been running, she announced she had been seeing to the unpacking of three new gowns delivered while she had been in Green Street that morning, and she was looking forward to some of that tea.

Tom and Farrie were close behind, both reporting on the unpacking of their clothing, and in short order all four were supplied with full cups.

Amelia joined Farrie on a small sofa made in the style of the drum chairs and linked her arm through that of her friend.

"It's going to be wonderful having you here." She gave a bright smile which included all the Sailings, before turning back to Farrie and lowering her voice slightly. "Wait until you hear my news!" Her look was so confidential Dorothea felt a slight qualm. Tom leaned forward, with an interested expression, but Amelia had turned back to Farrie. "Come up to my room and we'll have a wonderful gossip while they are unpacking your things."

"Are you going to keep secrets?" Tom demanded, stung at not being included.

"Of course we are," Amelia answered as if any gabby should understand. "You and Charlie keep them, don't you?"

"We don't have any," he said, more offended than ever at being left out.

"Well, you will," she replied with the air of a young woman who understood all such things. "Besides, you're to go across the garden and have a late lunch with Charlie, and we'll have a cold collation upstairs. Since we were working, we didn't get to go to Grillions." She tossed her golden curls and gave Dorothea a pert smile.

The door had been closed on the young ladies' exit for more than two minutes before Dorothea, caught up in the rush of the day, realized Tom was still staring at it with disappointment.

"Never mind," she said to him kindly. "She's right, you know. Soon you'll have all sorts of knowledge you won't want to tell them. In fact, you probably already do."

"What?" Tom looked interested as if Dorothea knew something he did not.

"I daresay you, Charlie and the Arnside gentlemen discussed all manner of things on your ride in the park this morning."

"Oh." Tom looked slightly uncomfortable and then shrugged. "I shouldn't think there was anything unfit for Farrie and Amelia to hear, and it would probably be boring to them, since we didn't discuss modistes and mantua makers." He straightened his shoulders, fingered his half-finished cup of tea and put it back on the table. "Think I'll wander next door. Wouldn't do to be late, since Charlie's probably sharp set and wanting his lunch," he said with a sudden air of nonchalance.

Dorothea watched him go and sat back in her chair, glad for a respite from the most harrowing day of her life. She had awakened to her financial problems, so usual in her life that she was almost comfortable with them. Just closing Lindsterhope House would alleviate many of them, but the strangeness of her new situation seemed to offset the advantages.

After her second solitary cup of tea she rose and, walking softly, left the drawing room and went out onto the landing to peer over the railing. Four men were just disappearing through the front door, carrying the buffet. All the unwanted luggage had vanished, as had most of the furniture from Green Street. It seemed that Mrs. Hicks was indeed a nonpareil among housekeepers.

THAT NEXT NIGHT at Lady Sefton's ball, Dorothea explained her feelings to Garreth as they watched their quartet of young people take to the floor for the first country dance.

"I'm persuaded that out of loyalty to Lord Wilton and Lady Harriet we mustn't mention her to a soul," she said. "I've no doubt they pay her well, but she is a pearl beyond price. She was so helpful in straightening out all the confusion that all the furniture was back where it belonged, our clothing was unpacked, and our dinner was excellent. There must be many who would offer her exorbitant sums to get their homes running so smoothly."

Before she had finished singing the praises of Mrs. Hicks, they were approached by a tall, lean man of fashion with laughing eyes looking out of a bored expression.

"Lord, is that really you, Tolver? I couldn't believe it when they told me you were finally back in town."

"Sopes." Garreth rose to meet the newcomer. "Didn't I hear you'd ascended to your father's place?"

"Probably. The old man shabbed off some three years ago."

"Then I'll introduce you to Lady Lindsterhope. Doro, this is the Earl of Sopewithy."

Dorothea rose and found the earl's eyes too disconcertingly sharp as they assessed her, but there seemed to be no hint of rudeness in his attitude, only a strangely deep interest. She was not to long undergo his attention, since after a pretty apology for intruding, he importuned Garreth to join him in the library where a group of their old friends had gathered.

"Talking about a trip up to Newmarket this week, all going together," he said. "Now that you're here, we'll have the old set back together again one more time."

Since Farrie was just coming off the dance floor after having taken a turn with Mr. Nelson and Lady

Amelia was returning with Lord Glissenton, who had
been avidly watching for her when they arrived that
evening, Dorothea was much too occupied to worry
about Garreth's temporary defection.

The group of "jolly sorts," as Tom and Charlie
were calling Miss Duval, her sister Susan and their
friends, had already gathered at the far end of the long
ballroom. Close to their watchful mamas, they were
standing in a group. Though they occupied their time
with amiable talk and hid their faces behind their fans
to suppress their twitters of laughter, they were nevertheless somewhat anxiously watching to see if Tom,
Charlie and their new companions, Eric and Lewis
Arnside, would remain when they returned their present partners from the floor.

Dorothea would not have been so disloyal to Tom
as to tell the young ladies that he and Charlie had in
one evening learned their liveliness far outweighed the
charms of a beauty like Miss Kettling, but she knew
the young ladies had nothing to fear. Not amorously
adventurous, the young men had found what they
considered a safe haven, and until they had forgotten
Miss Kettling's snub, they would be wary of risking
another.

"Lady Lindsterhope?" Someone spoke Dorothea's name, and she looked up quickly to see a stout
woman standing just to her left. The heavily jowled
face was vaguely familiar, doubtless half-remembered
from her first season so long ago. Her confusion must
have registered, because the woman took a seat on the
next rout chair which lined the wall and smiled with
understanding.

"You don't remember me, of course. After just coming back to town, you must be seeing so many new faces. You probably don't remember coming to a ball I gave for one of my nieces that year, but I will presume on that circumstance to renew our acquaintance."

"But of course I remember..." Dorothea said, hoping the other would help her to fill in the blanks in her memory. And though the lady did not speak and seemed slightly offended at not being remembered, she unwittingly prodded Dorothea's recollection by the quite offensive shade of her purple satin overskirt. A memory of a walk up a stairway to greet a hostess in a dreadful shade of burnt orange brought back a face which clearly showed the tendency to sag as the sixteen intervening years had proved it would. With it came a name.

"Your ball was one of the events of that year, Lady Ruston."

"What an excellent memory you have, my dear," the viscountess remarked, clearly impressed, but showed the ruthlessness of her reputation sixteen years before when she was known to be on the watch for husbands for her daughters. It was said that with three sisters, all of whom had made less-than-brilliant marriages and were producing numerous daughters, she would be at it for years to come. She came to the point of her decision to renew her acquaintance with Dorothea.

"I declare, seeing you and Lord Tolver together takes me back so many years. Old friendships don't die, do they, my dear?"

"Some do, but we are fortunate to be able to keep others," Dorothea answered placidly, though she could feel a chill moving in on her emotions. She could tell what was coming next.

"I am so sorry that dreadful old Lord Eanes kept me in conversation until Lord Tolver was called away. I had hoped to renew two acquaintances at the same time. You must bring Lord Tolver over to say hello directly he returns," she said rising. She affected to see someone on the other side of the room, gave a slight nod and took her leave.

Dorothea was watching her cross the room when she chanced to see Sally approaching from the right. Without a word, Lady Jersey took a seat, her eyes also following Lady Ruston.

"I would have headed her off if I could," Lady Jersey said without preamble. "I hope you gave her the go-by."

"Why should I?" Dorothea asked, knowing full well what Sally meant.

"Garreth's fortune is considerable, and there are a lot of hopeful mamas here who know it."

Dorothea had seen other speculating eyes turned on Garreth, and she had no doubts that lures would soon be strewn across his path. She doubted that she, a widow far beyond what was considered the ideal age for marriage would long hold his attention, but she could not tell Lady Jersey that.

"Sally, if Garreth has stayed a bachelor all these years, he's likely to remain one."

"You must warn him of one thing," Lady Jersey said, speaking with unwonted quiet. "Lady Ruston has never yet failed to get the gentleman she chooses for that veritable horde of nieces. She's married off eight of them, and there's some question about how she managed three.''

"Sally!''

"Recently she's been trying to ensnare young Mr. Gresham, and that poor fool's so besotted with Miss Edwards that he doesn't even see what's going on. I wonder sometimes how people can be so blind.''

"I have a problem believing people could do such things,'' Dorothea said, knowing her friend might deprecate her provincial attitudes. "I also wonder that you don't give the poor man a hint.''

"It isn't possible to protect everyone,'' Sally said. "But if you have any concern for Garreth, keep him widely separated from that woman. She's capable of anything.''

After a commonplace or two, Sally rose and left Dorothea to her thoughts. Did she need to warn Garreth, and if so, how did she go about it? He would not take kindly to the suggestion that he could not handle his own affairs. Moreover, his insufferable attitude that everyone and everything must move as he directed could blind him to the fact that he was being manipulated.

She had once heard her father say that two types of people were the most easily fleeced: the truly innocent and those who regarded themselves invulnerable because of their intellect.

Moreover Garreth was so much interested in protecting Charlie he might never think of himself as the quarry.

CHAPTER EIGHT

LADY JERSEY HAD NOT REACHED the end of the room before Dorothea decided against following her friend's advice. It would be the outside of enough if she interfered with Garreth's life. He was not the same young blade who had first stepped into society, and if a man was ever able to take care of himself, Viscount Tolver was one.

Moreover, anything she said could be taken as jealousy, and nothing would be more disastrous. Across the room, she could see Lady Ruston in conversation with a young woman who was certainly attractive enough to rouse that unworthy emotion in another female far less interested in Garreth than Dorothea.

And in truth she had little time to think of it, because at that moment she was approached by a portly gentleman she had known slightly in her first season. The intervening sixteen years had added considerably to his girth, and his white hair set off his somewhat high complexion. A park saunterer, she thought, judging by the high, starched collar points and the ornate configuration of his neckcloth, both of which had begun to wilt. He stopped in front of her and raised his quizzing glass, staring down at her, inadvertently favouring her with a picture of a gentleman who, while otherwise even featured, had a grotesquely enlarged left eye.

"Lady Lindsterhope," he wheezed, bowing over her hand. "Bless me, bless me. Could have been yesterday I saw you in town, yes it could, yes it could. Haven't changed a bit, not a bit."

"Thank you, Mr. Cheyney," Dorothea answered with a smile, though the gentleman could not know it was one of relief in remembering his name rather than one of welcome. The quizzing glass had been the prod that jogged her mind. She remembered him for that odiously discomfitting way he had of looking over a female as if he were checking a piece of fabric for flaws or inspecting a cut of meat to ascertain its freshness.

She chided herself on her inelegant thoughts and tried to give him a genuine smile, realizing she should be grateful for being remembered after being so long out of society; it would be most uncomfortable to have to begin again as a complete stranger. Moreover, Mr. Cheyney was a gentleman moving in the highest circles; his name often appeared in the society columns as one of those staying at the Pavillion in Brighton.

That thought gave her no pleasure. The cronies of the Prince were notorious for their debts, and gossip had it that several were hanging out for wealthy wives. She felt a stab of irritation over the talk about her dowry and wondered who had started the rumours which put her in such an unenviable position.

He appeared to take her smile as an invitation to join her, and eased his bulk onto a rout chair, which groaned under his weight, but he took no notice of it.

"Glad to see you back in town," he said, nodding as if approving his approval. "Telling the Regent just the other day, we can't have, no, we really can't have, too many beautiful women in society."

"I'm flattered that you include me in that group," Dorothea said, unable to hide the trace of a blighting tone. She had never overcome her distrust of such fulsome compliments, and wondered how long she would have to endure Mr. Cheyney's.

She was watching the country dance then in progress, noticing with some relief the easy conversation going on between Tom and Miss Duval, who topped him by nearly a head. They would not have been considered the most handsome couple on the floor even without the difference in height, but as the steps of the dance brought them together, they exchanged comments, smiled with pure enjoyment and seemed oblivious to the disparity that would have made many couples most uncomfortable.

Nor did Miss Duval seem the same young lady Dorothea had first noticed in Almack's. Standing by her mother and sister, her obvious anxiety over being left standing and ignored had accentuated her gangliness and narrow pinched face. Her enjoyment of Tom's company and the dance had softened her features until she was almost pretty, and she moved with an unself-conscious grace. An extremely tall young gentleman in the next set was watching her as the pattern of the dance allowed.

Though of course she could not have known it, Dorothea considered that Miss Kettling had accomplished a good night's work when she snubbed Charlie and put his back up. Had she been nicer at the outset, Tom and Charlie might have been part of the group that stood disconsolately to the side watching

the beauty on the floor with a gentleman who doubtless thought himself fortunate at the moment, but
would in all likelihood spend the rest of the evening
cast into the doldrums.

Charlie was dancing with the younger Miss Duval,
Sarah, whose plump little feet were having trouble
keeping up with his long steps. Dorothea thought she
must find a way to gently remind him to be more considerate of his partner, though the young lady seemed
to be bearing up well under the strain.

"Dreadful crush, dreadful crush," Mr. Cheyney
was saying. "As I said to the Regent, the Seftons are
far, far too good-natured, seem to invite just anyone
they meet. Not a good idea, not a good idea at all."

"I'm quite sure you're right," Dorothea said, not
having heard the first part of the conversation, for
Tom had said something to his partner which had included a fit of the twitters, and her attention had been
on the edge of the floor, hoping Sally had not found
cause to complain of their behaviour.

Not until he stopped directly in front of her did she
notice Lord Ingleforth, who stared down at Mr.
Cheyney as if affronted by the gentleman's presence.

"Good evening, Lady Lindsterhope. The evening is
a bit warm, so I brought you a glass of lemonade."

"Why, thank you, my lord," Dorothea murmured,
thinking she would rather do without the refreshment
than bear his company again, though she chided herself for her censure of a gentleman whose only noticeable fault was being on all points a person one did not
notice at all. Like Mr. Cheyney, he also took a seat
without invitation, sitting on the other side of her and
asking her how her day had gone.

"I'm sure you must find it rather gay with two young people about the house," he said, though his eyes as he viewed the dance floor seemed to take no pleasure in the youth at the ball.

"We are forever on the go," Dorothea answered, glad he had not discovered she was sojourning at Wilton House, a situation which brought her number of charges to three.

"Young people, ah, young people." Mr. Cheyney gave a sigh. "Remember the time, that wonderful time, when we used to spend our energies on such dances, Lady Lindsterhope?"

"I do indeed," she replied, wondering if he thought her in her infirm years, and her spirits lowered. All she needed was for someone to refer to her as a positive dragon, and her day would be complete. Perhaps she should have taken a rest that afternoon.

The country air had come to a halt, and she watched as young Captain Richardson of the Light Guard led Amelia off the floor, followed by Lieutenant Matthews, the even younger officer who escorted Farrie. Fleetingly Dorothea wondered if Lady Harriet approved of young officers, though the Light Guard was made up of the sons of some of the best families. The two couples came to stand just beyond Lord Ingleforth's chair, properly close to the young ladies' chaperon without interrupting the conversation in progress.

"I doubt Lady Lindsterhope has forgotten our dance the other night," Lord Ingleforth was saying, as if he had taken exception to Mr. Cheyney's remark.

The officers seemed disposed to exchange partners for the next dance, but they were suddenly inter-

rupted by the arrival of Lord Glissenton, who bowed
to Amelia and made some bantering comment to the
guardsmen which Dorothea missed, though it brought
a laugh from the gentlemen and Amelia. Apparently
Farrie enjoyed the joke, because her eyes were shining.

"Oh, I daresay kicking up the heels is good for the
constitution once in a while, once in a while." Mr.
Cheyney waved a negligent hand.

"Well, we have been given permission by Lady Jersey, so there," Amelia was saying as she made a pretty
moue and tossed her head for the benefit of Lord
Glissenton.

"But when one reaches maturity, true maturity, my
boy, one doesn't..." Mr. Cheyney was continuing, but
Dorothea only caught a snatch of the conversation
going on across her, because Lord Glissenton was answering Amelia.

"Then if Lady Jersey has given her permission, I
know Lady Lindsterhope will not be so callous as to
break my heart by refusing me your hand for this
dance."

Wouldn't she? Doro thought, not at all pleased with
his attentions to Lady Amelia, though in all fairness
the blame rested with Amelia and Lady Harriet. Of
what could the woman have been thinking to let her
daughter start a mild flirtation with a gentleman sim-
ply to get revenge on Miss Kettling for snubbing
Charlie? The situation would not have been to her
liking if the countess had been on hand to see that
Amelia kept to the line. But allowing the girl to go her
way and then leaving Dorothea to manage was unconscionable.

And if the situation were not bad enough, she shivered as if something vile had touched her and looked up to see Lady Kettling glaring at her from across the ballroom.

"Well, I daresay Lady Lindsterhope has not reached her dotage and still enjoys the waltz," Lord Ingleforth was saying, his voice rising slightly as if giving proof *he* was not one of advanced age; indeed, his petulance denied his maturity.

Dorothea had been on the point of telling Lord Glissenton that she felt the young officer had a prior claim on Lady Amelia's next dance. Behind Lord Glissenton and Amelia, Captain Richardson had taken Farrie's hand, and though too well mannered to break into the conversation, he was awaiting an opportunity to lead her onto the floor. Farrie had given her chaperon a questioning look she knew well, and Dorothea had nodded.

Too late she realized Lord Glissenton had taken her permission to Farrie and her officer to be for him, and he led Amelia away.

"Oh, drat," she muttered as the two couples moved away.

"Exactly what I say," Lord Ingleforth remarked, sitting back with a smug smile, and too late Dorothea realized Mr. Cheyney had been expounding again, but in her concern over her charges she had not heard a word. Since Lord Ingleforth took her utterance to be a comprehensive condemnation of Mr. Cheyney's opinion, she expected the portly gentleman to take some offence and was sunk in distress, but instead he smiled benignly and patted her hand in a fatherly manner.

"But it is delightful, truly delightful, my dear Lady Lindsterhope, to find a lady of your grace and poise still so full of the enthusiasm of youth."

She could not help but gaze wide-eyed as she wondered what she had missed, but Lord Ingleforth was rising from his seat. She expected him to take his leave, but he bowed gracefully.

"And to prove that wonderful enthusiasm, Lady Lindsterhope, would you honour me with this dance?"

"Oh, I really don't think..." She didn't finish the sentence, because on the dance floor she saw Charlie and Tom partnering two young ladies who were dressed identically in purple-flowered muslin frocks. If the young men were not actually turning the dance into a romp, their enthusiastic steps were not at all what the patronesses of Almack's would think proper. She had little hope of catching their eyes from the sidelines, but perhaps on the floor she would have a better opportunity.

"Thank you, Lord Ingleforth," she said, rising. "I hope I will not put you to the blush. The waltz was not in fashion when I was last in London."

Mr. Cheyney did not appear to like it when she rose, but he made a quick recovery. "I'm sure you will put every other lady to shame, Lady Lindsterhope."

But Dorothea did have an acquaintance with the dance. It gave her little pleasure to think she owed her knowledge to Sir Gerald and his sister, Elsa. They had instructed Tom and Farrie, and Tom's disinclination to put his feet to music had caused Dorothea to learn the dance to give him additional lessons. By the time he had gained confidence she was well versed in the steps. She paid little or no attention to the dance as she looked for an opportunity to pass a quelling look to Tom or Charlie.

"In one thing I do concur with Mr. Cheyney," Lord Ingleforth said, and Dorothea looked up, a question in her eyes.

"And what might that be, my lord?"

"That you do put the other ladies to shame."

"But you will put me to the blush, my lord," she said, dropping her eyes, her pretended confusion a good excuse for watching for Tom.

It was in fact Charlie who was the first to meet her gaze, and so forbidding a look did she give him that he coloured slightly and immediately corrected his steps. As Lord Ingleforth guided her a few steps farther, she saw Tom, who had apparently received a warning from Charlie's behaviour and he, too, was dancing with exaggerated propriety.

Lord Ingleforth was keeping up a running comment as they danced, leaving her no opening to speak, so she endeavoured to nod now and again and let his words go right over her head. A turn in the dance brought the double doorway into her view just as Lady Jersey entered the room, and she sighed, congratulating herself on bringing the boys to heel before Sally saw their antics.

But her elation was short-lived because, near the doorway, Garreth was bowing over the hand of the young female who appeared to be in Lady Ruston's charge, the one Dorothea had thought to be the niece.

He had apparently solicited her hand for the dance, because she rose, and Dorothea felt a stab of doubt as she saw the young woman was not only elegantly dressed, but of a willowy height that helped her to fit into the circle of Garreth's arm as if she had been designed for the purpose. Dorothea sighed for her own lack of inches and pulled her eyes away from the tortuous spectacle. If anyone were capable of putting the other ladies in the shade by her grace on the floor, it was Lady Ruston's niece, and that was just too much to endure.

To Dorothea, that waltz seemed to be interminable, and when it ended she was heartily in agreement with Mr. Cheyney that dancing should be left to the young.

Lord Ingleforth led her back to her chair, beside which Mr. Cheyney sat, patiently waiting. As she took her seat he nodded ponderously as if passing on some sombre judgement.

"As I suspected, Lady Lindsterhope, just as I suspected. You are indeed the most graceful lady on the floor tonight. Does a man good to see a female who understands the graces of times past."

"Thank you, sir," she answered, not sure his compliment was at all flattering in this case. Was he equating her with the ladies who made their comeout in his youth? She had not even been born at the time. Really, she must start taking a rest in the afternoons before these strenuous evening engagements.

"Lady Lindsterhope," Lord Ingleforth said, leaning forward slightly to speak around her, "is a superb example of grace of *her own time*. Being a *part* of it, I consider myself a fair judge."

"Oh, dear," Dorothea murmured faintly, but neither gentleman took any notice.

To further emphasize his words, Lord Ingleforth raised his quizzing glass and trained it on the aging rake. Not to be put down by a mere halfling a score of years his junior, Mr. Cheyney brought up his own ocular weaponry and stared back. Dorothea found herself flanked by two hideously enlarged left eyes, one a washed-out and bloodshot blue, the other a nondescript brown.

Dorothea thought that if this was the quality of suitors she ranked, no wonder Garreth had sought more enlivening company.

"I daresay *some*, I say, *some* people can consider themselves *judges* of a time in which they were not born and can know nothing about," Mr. Cheyney remarked with a loftiness meant to put Lord Ingleforth in his place.

But the baron had no intention of giving up the field. "And I daresay after her seclusion, Lady Lindsterhope is looking forward to spending time in the company of companions *her own age*."

"Do you know, it is dreadfully hot in here," Dorothea said breathlessly, opening her fan and wielding it vigorously, but the battle was fairly joined now, and neither gentleman seemed to hear her. Never had she ever considered the possibility of bringing out such an ardour in a suitor that a scene could develop, and she had no clear idea of what to do about it. All she could think of was escape.

"I think you will find, *my dear boy*—" Mr. Cheyney continued laying out his insinuations more sparingly, but using them on what he considered the lord's vulnerability "—that by the time a lady has reached the age of sensible thought, she sees more value in *social prestige* than in a *romp* around the dance floor.''

Dorothea was ready to sink, wondering how much her normally strong nerves could stand when an opportunity to escape presented itself. Captain Richardson and Farrie approached from her left, and through the throng of guests gathering around the end of the room came Amelia and Lord Glissenton.

''Excuse me, but I must speak with Lady Amelia and my ward,'' she murmured and rose quickly before either gentleman had the presence of mind to stop her, but neither made any move to do so. She wondered if it was merely the imaginings of her overset nerves, or if, as it seemed, their only response had been a flicker in their eyes as their sustained glares were interrupted by her passing.

She stepped down the room past several empty chairs as if she were leaving Lord Ingleforth and Mr. Cheyney a bit of privacy for their talk, and waited pointedly for the young ladies to join her. Amelia had been in animated conversation with Lord Glissenton, but she seemed not at all adverse to giving some time to her chaperon.

''My dear, you look flushed,'' Dorothea said, feeling as false as the two gentlemen she had left. ''I wonder if you should not sit down and rest a bit.'' She glanced up at Lord Glissenton, wondering how she could politely hint him away, but he had turned to speak to Farrie.

''. . . And if Lady Lindsterhope will allow, I will be honoured if you would keep the next waltz for me,'' he was saying.

All Dorothea's protective instincts rose to choke her,
and she wanted to tell the young lord to take himself
off. How dare he use Farrie to stay close to Amelia?
She could still hear Lady Harriet's warning to her
daughter that Lord Glissenton was well enough, but
not her sort, and if he was not eligible for Amelia, he
was not going to break Farrie's heart. But Farrie was
looking at her with a face glowing with hope, and
Dorothea could only nod dumbly.

As Lord Glissenton walked away, Amelia's eyes
twinkled. "Do I perceive, dear Doro, that you are
coming down with a severe headache?"

After Mr. Cheyney's remarks about her age, Dorothea thought she must look the most haggish woman
in the room if even the young ladies had noticed
something amiss. Then she saw Amelia's speaking
look in the direction of the two gentlemen who were
still embroiled in their argument, doing verbal battle
across a vacant chair.

While expressing her indignation might give vent to
her pent-up feelings, she would set a poor example for
her charges, so she suggested they sit for a moment
and compose themselves for the dancing to come.

"I've no objection," Amelia said with a frank sigh.
"Just first let me see what that scamp Charlie is
about."

"He is being quite the beau," Dorothea said, and
found herself speaking only to Farrie since Amelia had
walked away a few paces, and was imperiously waving at the young marquess. She had caught his attention and as usual he had taken instant and warm
exception to her demanding his company. He frowned
and shook his head stubbornly, which only caused her

to toss her own head and set her curls to bobbing as she made an even more demanding gesture.

"She must not do that," Dorothea said, ready to rise from her seat and go after Amelia. "Obviously he does not want to come."

"He will," Farrie said, and was almost immediately proved right as Charlie started around the edge of the room, his expression mulish.

"At first I was concerned for both of them," Farrie went on. "But now I am persuaded he takes as much pleasure in thwarting Amelia as she does in ordering him about. If they behaved normally they would think each other sadly out of frame."

"But it presents such an off appearance," Dorothea objected. "I'm convinced others will not understand." Despite her concern, she remained in her seat, hoping Charlie and Amelia would know better than to break into a childish quarrel in the middle of a ball. After a hot remark, pitched too low to be heard even two paces away, Charlie listened to Amelia, nodded and strolled away. She returned to join Dorothea and Farrie where she gratefully took a chair and threatened to kick off her slippers.

Farrie was quick of wit, but when her mind was otherwise occupied she often missed a teasing remark, and not realizing Amelia was cutting a wheedle for her benefit, was vigorously explaining why she could not remove her shoes.

It was at that point that Garreth strolled over.

"Haven't you fobbed these two off on anyone yet?" he demanded, glancing down at Amelia and Farrie and then turning back to her. "I think you're promised to me for supper."

"We're promised to Captain Richardson and Lieutenant Matthews," Amelia said with a toss of her head. "You needn't think we'll foist ourselves on you."

"Then I wish they'd come and get you, because I'm devilish sharp set and I want to go in to supper before this dance ends." He turned his head and nodded, and Dorothea looked to see the two young officers hovering near by. His permission seemed to be all that had held them back and they came forward with alacrity.

With the two young couples strolling in front of them, Garreth and Dorothea made their slow way around the dance floor toward the dining room. Garreth grinned down at her. "Going the pace, aren't you, old girl? Two suitors glaring at each other? Just think of it, you will be the subject of a scandal if one calls the other out."

She looked back over her shoulder where Mr. Cheyney and Lord Ingleforth were still in discussion and shook her head.

"I was truly set up in my own conceit, thinking I was the cause of their disagreement, but I have been put in my place for my pride. I've no doubt they do not yet know I'm gone."

"Poor Doro, I should have kept a closer eye on you, but I was busy securing invitations for us for the Ruston affair."

"Oh?" She quite thought he had been otherwise engaged, but thought better of saying so.

"Ruston is a different sort, part of this new set of gentlemen farmers. I thought Charlie and Tom might pick up some interesting ideas. Won't be long before they'll be running their own estates."

"Quite true," she said, not ready to totally accept his explanation, but she had something else on her mind.

"I'm concerned about Amelia," she began slowly, not at all sure how to say what she felt must be said. "I don't really care for her attentions to Lord Glissenton."

"Flirting, is she?" he looked up, his eyes following the young lady as she walked with Lieutenant Matthews. "It's to be expected, a chit as pretty as she's become. Don't let her worry you."

"But I heard Lady Harriet warn Amelia he was not her sort, as she put it."

"Lord, no, he'd never do for Amelia, but she won't make talk for herself. If she seems to be going beyond the line I'll call her back."

His words would have been reassuring if she had not looked up just then to see him give a nod and a smile to Lady Ruston and her niece, who were standing in conversation with Lady Sefton.

He seemed overly taken with the matchmaker's attractive young relative, and Dorothea wondered if he would have time for Amelia or anyone else at Wilton House.

CHAPTER NINE

THE MORNING AFTER the Sefton ball, Dorothea awoke with a sense of bemusement, unable to account for her surroundings. Then with a rush, the events of the day before came back to her, and looming largest and out of place in the chain of happenings was the attraction Garreth had shown for Juliet Oglesby, Lady Ruston's niece. Lady Maria Kettling had made it her business to see that Dorothea could put a name to her rival, as if she needed that final bit of information to be convinced of trouble ahead.

Lady Sefton's ball had been the recognized opening of the season, but as usual, the schedule of activities began sporadically, much like the new arrival who bravely steps through the door and then pauses, not sure whether to stride forward with purpose or siddle around the wall. Dorothea found her social calendar empty of engagements for the next two days.

Garreth had assured her that with the demand for London housing during the season, his man of business could find an immediate tenant for Lindsterhope House. Nevertheless, a few mornings later, she was much surprised to receive a visit from him with the signed lease for the season and a cheque for the entire amount. The speed was accounted for by the tenant's already having leased a house on Mount Street, which had suffered a fire while the family was on the way to London. They had been grateful to find any place readily available.

With her finances in better tune, Dorothea took Farrie to Bond Street for the dress she had so desired, and once back at Wilton House, both Sailings ladies settled themselves to their needlework. Amelia, with surprising efficiency, settled herself to make a list of the acceptances of the Easterly-ball invitations, and discussed with Mrs. Hicks the preparations, which were even then under way.

While the ladies were thus occupied, Tom and Charlie left to join Eric and Lewis Arnside and a party of their friends for the evening. Though Dorothea worried, Garreth had assured her that the young Arnsides were unexceptional, so she said nothing, deciding she should be grateful that Tom seemed willing enough to spend so much of his time escorting his sister and herself to social activities most young men scorned.

But by late morning of the second day, she was becoming heartily bored. Mrs. Hicks did in fact have the Wilton house so much in order that Dorothea seldom caught a glimpse of a maid, an ash boy, nor indeed even the housekeeper, who had been so much in evidence when they had first arrived. Used to the exigencies of her own dithery Mrs. Marks, the perfection of Wilton House left something to be desired.

She was therefore relieved to hear the front door knocker and the subsequent tread of Jenkins, the Easterly's butler, as he came toward the door of the morning room. She waited expectantly as he opened the door and made his announcement.

"Lord Glissenton and Mr. Baskin Haworth, my lady."

Dorothea hastily thrust aside her sewing and rose. The stab of irritation over learning Lord Glissenton had arrived was totally overborne by her delight in the second visitor.

"Baskin!" She went forward, holding out her hands to the gentleman who, next to Garreth and Sally, had been the dearest friend of her younger days.

The Honourable Mr. Baskin Haworth was just above medium height, with deep auburn hair, dancing blue eyes and a clear, but vivid, complexion. Happily he had outgrown his childhood infirmities which had prevented him from taking part in energetic games. When he was nearing his twentieth year he had travelled to his family's holdings in India and South Africa, and had since spent most of his time out of the country. Unlike Garreth, he had been a regular correspondent, so she knew he had only just returned to England.

He came striding across the room, taking her hands and smiling down into her face.

"Doro, you wretch! There I was camping on your doorstep in Green Street until Lord Glissenton took pity on me."

"Oh, no, did you?" she crowed, too glad to see him to worry over whether or not he was exaggerating the case.

"I called there yesterday and found the knocker off the door," he said, leading her back to the sofa where she had been sitting and then joined her there, still holding her right hand. "I was so sure I had the wrong address that I went back to the hotel, checked and returned to Green Street. If I had not discovered Glissenton at White's, I would not yet know what had happened. Have I told you that you are as lovely as ever?''

''No, only reminded me that I am sadly remiss as a hostess,'' she remarked, recalling he had been accompanied by Lord Glissenton. She turned to greet their other visitor, but he was in jesting conversation with Amelia and Farrie.

She had hardly begun the introductions when the door opened again and Tom and Charlie who strolled into the room looking somewhat disconsolate.

''Strawberries for luncheon,'' Charlie stated after the introductions, as if the circumstances boded some ill wind. ''Must mean Garreth is not coming back today.''

''Pho,'' Amelia said, tossing her head. ''You know Mrs Hicks always gets them for you when they're in season.'' She turned to Dorothea. ''They're his favourites.''

''She always used to get strawberries when one of Garreth's business trips was delayed,'' Charlie said, still aggrieved.

''He's not on a business trip now,'' Dorothea said, trying to soothe the young marquess. ''And you could hardly expect him to reach home before tea.''

''Finding London a bit flat?'' Baskin asked, his eyes twinkling. ''I used to when I was your age.''

''I don't know why, after raking about town last night with a new group of friends,'' Amelia said, her censure a cover for a slight wounding of feelings when she learned Charlie was moving into a circle in which she could not go.

"Mind your tongue, Amelia," Charlie said, rounding on her. "Going to Cribbs Parlour and the Daffy Club is not raking, which you don't know anything about, anyway."

"Then neither do you nor Tom," she retorted.

"Didn't say we did." Charlie came back at her and looked as if he might say more, but he wasn't allowed to continue. Baskin turned to Tom with a twinkle in his eye.

"Daffy Club, eh? Is it still the same, I wonder?"

Tom looked extremely conscious, and Charlie, turning quickly from his argument with Amelia, stepped into the conversation.

"Daresay it is, but since it was our first time, we don't know what it was like before. Lively enough, wouldn't you say, Tom?"

"Lively," Tom said, seemingly relieved to be given a hint.

Dorothea watched the young baron with concern. Had something happened at the Daffy Club? she wondered. Rumour had it that young men often overimbibed gin, which they called blue ruin, and afterward cut up larks like boxing the watch. She wondered if Tom had landed himself in some minor scrape, but knew better than to ask.

While Lord Glissenton continued his conversation with Amelia and Farrie, Baskin kept the young men in conversation, and with a speed she would have expected only from Garreth, ascertained what had brought about their collective megrims.

"Yes, society does seem to be confining, expecting you to ride in the mornings or only after tea, and never to gallop in the park," he said. "After a few days in town, I know I feel the need to do something." He leaned forward a little. "I wouldn't want this to get out or someone would think I'm a flat, but I think I'll go to the Exeter Exchange this afternoon. Want to see if the tigers from India are as big as the ones you see in the wild."

"That would be interesting," Charlie said, his eyes lighting, but suddenly wary as if he might be showing too much enthusiasm. "Good thing to know. Having been out to the colonies and all, you'd be able to judge."

Apparently Lord Glissenton's conversation had not been absorbing enough to hold Amelia's entire attention. She leaned forward in her chair, her tone imperious.

"Don't think you're going to the Exeter Exchange and leave us at home, Charlie Landruth."

"Well, why not make a party of it and we'll all go?" Tom suggested. "I daresay Doro is as interested in the animals as we are... Uh, that is, if Mr. Haworth doesn't mind us—"

Baskin spoke up quickly. "Glad to have you. It's not much fun alone, and there's something else I'm interested in while we're about it. I don't know what possessed them to bring Napoleon's carriage back to London, but I'll not be the only one in town not to see it."

This second suggestion so exactly fitted with the interests of Tom and Charlie that they immediately pressed Mr. Haworth and Lord Glissenton to remain for luncheon and the party could start out immediately afterward.

Seven was an awkward number, but Lord Glissenton solved the problem by suggesting that Tom and Farrie ride with him in his tilbury while the other four followed in the Easterly carriage. Dorothea reluctantly agreed, though she wondered if Lord Glissenton might be enlisting the sympathy of Farrie and Tom in his pursuit of Amelia. She was sure of it when she learned he had allowed Tom to drive the tilbury, after which the young Baron pronounced him a very good fellow indeed.

If Dorothea found the animals at the Exchange a bit uninteresting, the four young people gaped just like the children who were being held firmly in tow by their nurses and tutors. Lord Glissenton, some five years older than Tom, and more accustomed to the sights of town, seemed to view the enthusiastic interest of the others with a gentle humour, but showed himself conversant on the wild beasts and their habitats.

"However did you know to suggest this?" Dorothea said as she accepted Baskin's arm and strolled along behind the others.

"It is so exactly what Tom and Charlie needed." She explained the marquess's close relationship to his guardian. "I believe it's come as a shock to him that Garreth can have friends of his own."

"Having three much younger brothers has given me an idea of what halflings are like when they're just beginning in society and still haven't quite shaken off the boy inside."

"Are your brothers in town?" Dorothea asked. "I confess, I don't remember them."

"Half brothers, my father's second wife," he explained. "They've taken over my work in India and on the plantation in Ceylon. Good sorts, really, much like those two."

"I imagine you miss them," Dorothea said, pleased that he found Tom and Charlie to his liking, but not wanting to comment on it.

"Not as much as you'll miss those two." He nodded his head toward where Tom and Farrie stood in discussion with Lord Glissenton. "It won't be long now before they're leading their own lives. Then what happens to you, Doro?"

"Oh, I'll contrive," she said, her voice suddenly tight.

"I think they've gaped enough," Mr. Haworth said easily as if he had not caught the catch in her voice. "We should be getting on to the Liverpool Museum or we'll be late in getting you back to tea."

The emperor's carriage was a disappointment to Dorothea and to the young ladies, for though it was of a moderate opulence, it did not fit their expectations of what the vehicle belonging to a man who'd planned to conquer all Europe should look like. It was soon plain that Tom and Charlie found something more. It was the closest they would come to the glory of war, and they were entranced when a chance remark led to the discovery that Lord Glissenton had fought in France. They stood staring at the carriage while he obligingly regaled them with the story of his experience in a battle.

On the return to Curzon Street, Amelia and Charlie rode in the tilbury with Lord Glissenton, a situation which Dorothea would have prevented if she could have found a way to do so. And while her concern for Amelia had cast a pall over the afternoon, she

was deeply gratified by Baskin's easy acceptance of her
wards, especially Tom, who had lacked and hungered
for a male mentor as a child, and who had not completely grown out of it. It was he who pressed Mr.
Haworth to take his tea with them, adding the invitation to Lord Glissenton, who left them at the door of
Wilton House after pleading a previous engagement.

They were in the drawing room, the boys devour-
ing a plate of sandwiches while Baskin answered in-
numerable questions from Charlie and Tom on the
animals of India, when the door opened and Garreth
strode into the room. He still wore his travelling
clothes, and though most of the mud of the journey
had been brushed away, some traces still remained.

"No tea over there, no lunch, and I'm devilish
hungry," he announced by way of explanation for his
sudden intrusion.

He ignored the babble of greetings from Amelia,
Tom, Farrie and Charlie and advanced straight toward the confidante where Dorothea was presiding
over the teapot. He had just reached her when he realized there was a sixth member of the party in the
person of Mr. Haworth.

"Hullo," he said, checking himself, surprised and
apparently not too pleased, though the slight frown
disappeared immediately he recollected himself.

Dorothea's introduction seemed to mean little to
him, and though he shook hands with a guise of amiability, his eyes contained a look of sharp speculation.

"I don't suppose you *do* remember me," Baskin
said easily as he sat back in his chair. "I recall you
from my visits to the Orchards. I'd see you and Doro

galloping off across the fields in the mornings. How I wanted to go with you."

Garreth's brow cleared as he took a seat by Dorothea on the sofa.

"Baskin, I do remember. You were..." He paused, as if not knowing how to go on.

"The sickly one," Baskin answered, grinning. "Fortunately it was one of those things one outgrows."

"He's been in India—" Charlie volunteered, only to be interrupted by Tom.

"And Ceylon and Africa."

Garreth and Baskin were given no more time to renew their acquaintance as Tom and Amelia vied with Charlie, who was determined to tell his guardian about their afternoon. Garreth let them talk, using the time to sate the worst of his hunger.

When they had exhausted the subject, Amelia demanded to know of Baskin if there was any sport to be had while riding on an elephant, and while the others listened to him explain hunting Indian-style, Garreth leaned back on the sofa after handing Dorothea his cup to be refilled.

"I ran on a bit of good luck," he said with a boyish grin. "My old chums are not so happy with me. I bested them in the buying of a horse. Wait till you see him."

"A hunter?" Dorothea enquired.

"No, but he's a prime beast—a grey. Charlie will go mad for him."

But Garreth's ward was at that moment giving all his attention to Baskin who was telling them about a tiger hunt. Garreth frowned at the man as if he were an interloper on the scene.

"When did he show up?" he asked under his breath. "What do you know about him?"

Dorothea turned a puzzled gaze on him. "He's my second cousin. He used to visit us when he was a boy. What more can I say?"

"Sure he's not a dirty dish? This business of being out of the country so much smacks of some old scandal."

"Of course not," she retorted, unable to understand Garreth's attitude. "The Haworths are highly respected, as well as being very well off. They have extensive properties out there."

"Then forget I said anything. I may be overly suspicious," he said, putting his cup back on the table. "Charlie, you've scoffed all the sandwiches, and you've probably been here every waking hour since I've been gone. It's time we gave Doro a rest from our company."

He rose and waited for his ward to gulp down his last tea and make his farewells. Dorothea watched them leave, wondering what had happened to make Garreth behave so oddly. She had noticed the unmistakable fatigue in his face. Perhaps the gathering of old friends had not gone as well as he had hoped. She knew they had planned to stay at an inn, and it could have been noisy, preventing him from getting his rest. After consideration, she could not think of anything else that might have upset him.

"Do you really m-mean it?" Tom was saying, so excited that his stutter had reappeared and brought Dorothea out of her thoughts.

"Of course you understand we won't be in the gymnasium." Baskin told him. "This is dinner and a lot of talk on the science of the sport. There'll be no putting on the gloves."

"I d-daresay there're not many who get to spend an evening hearing Gentleman Jackson talk!"

"What's this?" Dorothea asked, looking curiously at their visitor.

"Mr. Haworth has invited me to go to dinner with Gentleman Jackson," Tom said as if he could hardly believe it.

Dorothea surveyed Mr. Haworth with surprise. "Baskin! I didn't know you were interested in pugilism."

"Not physically," the gentleman answered with a smile. "When I was younger I didn't have enough weight to stand up against a windstorm, so I spent my time watching and analysing. Gentleman Jackson took pity on me and helped me to understand what I was seeing. I've been collecting data on the different methods of fighting and wrestling in my travels. That's what we mean to discuss tonight."

Tom turned anxious eyes on her. "We don't have anything planned for tonight, do we, Doro?"

"No, nothing," she said, laughing at him. "And though it's probably only the female in me, I would much rather you meet a man of that sort over a dining table than in the sport itself."

But though she had made light of her objections to the sport of boxing, Dorothea could not rest easy over the idea of Tom's being drawn into that circle. She had never known him to have any interest in the more violent sports, but he had quickly taken to her cousin, and could be led into them.

She had just finished dressing for dinner when Farrie came into her room. One look at Miss Sailings's face and Dorothea knew the young lady was worried, though she did not seem in deep distress. After Myra had helped drape her mistress's shawl about her shoulders, Dorothea sent the maid away and waited. Farrie was not long in bringing up her worries.

"I wish Tom had not gone out," she said quietly. "I wanted to talk to him."

"We could not have prevented him," Dorothea said. "He might even have the advantage on the Arnside gentlemen in being a part of tonight's discussion. To try to stop him would have been too selfish of us."

"I'm not even sure he wanted to go," Farrie said. "Something has been wrong with him today."

"I thought he enjoyed himself enormously." Dorothea looked back on the day, which had seemed to be all excitement and wonder for Tom.

"I know, it was as if he were grabbing at things to see, to do..." Farrie shrugged. "Perhaps I am imagining trouble, but it seemed to me he was not himself."

"He has been bored and overly excited by turns," Dorothea said quietly. "For his sake I hope you are reading more into the situation than is there."

"I could be," Farrie answered, fingering the fringe on her shawl. "Lord Glissenton said something in passing that overset my peace."

"Good heavens! What pray?" Perhaps she should give that young lord his congee.

"Oh, nothing in the least offensive," Farrie hastened to reassure her guardian when she saw her expression. "While we were viewing the emperor's carriage, he mentioned to Amelia that the hero of that battle, Sir Gerald, had returned to London."

When Farrie left her, Dorothea sat down on the stool in front of her dressing table and tried to reconstruct the day with her focus on Tom's behaviour. She remembered his slavish attention to Lord Glissenton's war story, and to nearly every word Baskin had said, but she had taken it to be the attention of a young man shut away in the country for too long and anxious to catch up with the world.

Her mind had been too much taken up with what she considered Amelia's danger in flirting with Lord Glissenton, and she had not paid much attention to Tom.

If she had been right about Sir Gerald's intentions, she might have been wrong to bring Tom to London. There were so many more traps in the city which an unsuspecting young man could be led into if he were in the wrong company. Perhaps she should speak to him, but if he resented it, if he felt she might be trying to hold him in leading strings, she might lose any chance she had of advising him when he needed it.

Garreth was good at handling young men, and she would talk to him about Sir Gerald, she thought. But what if she were wrong about the man? She could be seriously maligning his character. And could she go to Garreth? He was behaving strangely, too.

Too many things were happening all at once, she decided. Too much around her was entirely escaping her understanding.

CHAPTER TEN

A FORTNIGHT LATER, Dorothea was to look back on the two days of social inactivity with a wistful sigh. She felt she needed the rest. Her days had been filled with shopping trips, for while Amelia was decisive and showed excellent taste, she preferred to have Dorothea accompany her on her shopping expeditions.

Sensible of her responsibility of chaperoning Lady Amelia, Dorothea planned her schedule for either strolling in the park or riding in the Easterly carriage every afternoon and let no important social activity pass without showing the young lady to the best possible advantage.

Yet it seemed to her that she had only to set foot out of the house with her charges to find Lord Glissenton in attendance on Amelia. How she was to explain that fact to Lady Harriet put her at a loss. She would have hinted him away, but he so carefully divided his attention between Amelia, Farrie, herself, Tom and Charlie when they were present, that there was nothing about which she could complain.

Nor was Lord Glissenton her main worry for Amelia's sake. Sir Gerald had indeed shown himself in London and had brought his sister, Elsa, with him. He had boasted of being received in society, and apparently it was true. They met him everywhere, and he was showing marked attention to Amelia.

Dorothea had pushed her doubts aside and had mentioned her fears about Sir Gerald to Garreth, but while he had agreed to keep a close eye on Tom, he waved away any idea that the Earl of Wilton's daughter might be in danger. It was to Farrie that Dorothea looked to for support. The shy young lady was making a valiant attempt to stay by Amelia's side.

As if her worries over Tom and Amelia weren't enough to vex her, Dorothea was having suitor problems of her own. Lord Ingleforth and Mr. Cheyney were just as assiduous, though the subjects of their continuing arguments had within a few days moved to sporting events, fashions, politics and the current editor of the Gazette, all carried on over her head.

Much to her surprise, Baskin Haworth had taken rooms in Mount Street and was joining wholeheartedly in the social season. His birth, fortune, eligibility and manners made him a gentleman much in demand by hostesses, though he had never spent much time in London. He was the one bright spot in the passing days.

One difficulty she had feared had not come to pass. After learning Sir Gerald was in London, she had worried over Tom every time he left the house, fearing the man she considered an adventurer would lead him into some scrape. But Tom was spending a great deal of time with Garreth and Charlie, and since Garreth had actually allowed him to ride Greythorne, his new and much prized mount, Tom could not see enough of Charlie's guardian. When the young baron was not with them or the Arnsides, he attached himself to Baskin Haworth. And while Dorothea could not like it that Tom was indeed gaining an interest in pugilism, Baskin's liking for the boy had led to Tom's receiving lessons with the great Gentleman Jackson himself.

As she had expected, Garreth's attention had begun to wane, and though from the first she knew it was inevitable, she could not care for his attentions to Miss Oglesby, who did seem to be clutching his arm at every opportunity and making it plain to all and sundry that she had a claim on him. Dorothea could not quite understand what she was seeing, for it did not appear to her that Garreth particularly sought the young woman out, rather that Lady Ruston was foisting both herself and her niece on him. Still, he seemed to be doing nothing to repel them.

In Curzon Street, where both he and Charlie ran tame in Wilton House as they had been wont to do when the earl and the countess were in residence, he was still the same, though Dorothea had begun to notice he most often found some reason to leave when Baskin Haworth was present. She could not understand his dislike for her second cousin.

Altogether, she was beginning to wish she had never found it necessary to make the trip to London. Her preference for the country found force at that particular moment because of her surroundings. She was strolling with Amelia and Farrie through a garden, one referred to as a Persian paradise, though from her reading, she doubted whether any native of Persia would have recognized it.

Doubtless the Duchess of Alverson had read something of the natural gardens of the East, but what she had accomplished at Reslon had at least, succeeded in resembling nature, due to the fact that her plants were thriving. And the effect was so restful, so peaceful that Dorothea found herself taking an inordinate pleasure in the garden and wondering if anything like it could be accomplished at Marvale.

"I do like the country!" Farrie announced, her voice so animated with wistfulness that Dorothea was brought out of her reverie.

"This isn't country," said Amelia, who walked with them. "There is just such a small dell close to Salvermain which I think could be made as pretty. I wish Mama were here to see it."

"I wish I had brought my sketchbook," Farrie said, looking around.

"You can't be sitting drawing at an alfresco breakfast," Amelia admonished her. "Still, if we put some effort into it, perhaps we can remember which plants the duchess has put together. We'll attempt to lay out a plan tomorrow morning."

Dorothea surveyed the two young ladies, glad they had the good sense to keep their reflections to themselves, because she was not at all certain the duchess would like to have her ideas copied and recreated, though she knew that was exactly what both Amelia and Farrie had in mind. It showed that they, also, were turning their minds toward home.

It wasn't until Farrie spoke of the country with such longing in her voice that Dorothea realized her ward had not come to accept the social activities as well as her growing composure suggested. A brave little soul, she had acquiesced to the trip for Tom's sake, and went to the dinners and balls because of Amelia, but her wistfulness warned Dorothea she really wanted nothing as much as to return to Marvale.

Hearing Farrie's unintentional plea was enough to set the seal on Dorothea's lowered spirits. It was bad enough that she herself was growing increasingly unhappy with London, and that Tom, a young man of sturdy good health at home, was looking increasingly drawn. Apparently the air of the city did not agree with him. Her conscience bothered her that it was Farrie and not herself who had first noticed the change in him. When moods of depression seemed to overtake him with increasing frequency, she had questioned him.

He had at first tried to pass it off as her imagination, and then admitted that he was finding it increasingly difficult to sleep. He indignantly refused to allow her to call in Sir William Knighton, who might have discovered the problem and given him some sleeping powders, saying his friends would learn of it and think him a flat. Though his expressed reasoning struck Dorothea as a put-off, she decided to forebear putting pressure on him, since in a few weeks they would be returning home.

As if thinking of him had brought him on the scene, he came hurrying toward them down a side path.

"They're bringing out the food. Charlie and Garreth are holding a place for us, but you'd better make haste," he said with no preamble to Farrie or Amelia, this latter, who, in less than a fortnight, had become a second sister.

"I don't see why we should rush because you and Charlie are always bottomless pits," Amelia, who was most interested in the paradise, retorted.

"Fine, dawdle as much as you want, and you'll end up sitting with Mr. Cheyney and Lord Ingleforth, because they're both lying in wait for Doro."

"I'd rather sit with Charlie and Uncle Garreth," Farrie said gently. She and Tom had never indulged in the sharp retorts that were so much a part of Amelia and Charlie's relationship. Neither was autocratic, demanding or obstinate, and was more used to giving in to the requests made by the other. In addition, Farrie was in lively fear of Mr. Cheyney's "ogle glass," as Tom called it in one of his lighter moods.

They left the dell and crossed the wide expanse of lawn to where several large tents were set up to shelter the tables, and were just passing the first when Tom looked ahead.

"Well of all the damn—if that isn't enough," he expostulated. "All we need is that Ruston woman and her niece at our table," he muttered as he led Dorothea toward one of the tents in the centre of the dining area.

She felt her spirits sink as she, too, looked to see a long table where Charlie and Garreth stood, and with them Lady Ruston and Miss Oglesby. Farrie and Amelia had already brought the group to six, and since it was well-known that Dorothea was their chaperon, there was nothing she could do but join the group.

Since Lady Ruston had found occasion to draw her niece and Garreth together without Dorothea's help, they had not met again, nor had she been introduced to Miss Oglesby.

Farrie and Amelia stood by the table, completely ignored by Lady Ruston and her niece while Miss Oglesby carried on an animated one-sided conversation with Garreth. As Dorothea approached she overheard the barest facts of how, on the way to the breakfast, Lord Dunsney's carriage had broken an axle, causing those following him to suffer a delay.

"He could have been considerate enough not to have brought that antiquated old wagon out when he knew the road would be so crowded," Miss Oglesby said as she opened her blue-and-white sunshade and twirled it flirtatiously.

Lord Dunsney had been a friend of Dorothea's and Garreth's family for years, an impoverished nobleman whose pride, dignity and honour had never been tarnished by his lean purse. Dorothea felt for the old gentleman; she could not see Garreth's face to judge his response to the young woman's callous remark. Either by accident or design, the parasol blocked her view.

"I trust the old gentleman hasn't suffered an injury," Dorothea said, too interested in Lord Dunsney's welfare to worry over what could have been an unintended slight. Nor did she like the amusement she saw in Garreth's eyes, as if he were so besotted with the lovely blonde that he had no concern for an old family friend. When Miss Oglesby was forced to turn and acknowledge her, it was obvious by the cold blue eyes and crisp answer that the young woman had known what she was doing with the sunshade.

"I wouldn't know," she answered, her tone cool as though she were suppressing some toad-eating mushroom.

By Dorothea's side, Tom stiffened, seeing the coolness of Miss Oglesby's remark as an insult to Doro.

His face must have given him away, because suddenly Amelia spoke up, her voice falsely light and loud.

"Lady Lindsterhope, since you're always considered the Mama of what Uncle Garreth considers the horde, won't you seat us so they can begin serving? Uncle Garreth, as temporary Papa, shouldn't you be at the head of the table?"

Dorothea had to suppress a gasp. It was enough that they must bear the atrocious manners of Miss Oglesby, but for Amelia to openly challenge her—for her remark could have no purpose but to put Lady Ruston and her niece in their places—would only make an embarrassing incident worse. Her gaze fluttered up to meet Garreth's, hoping for his assistance, but his eyes still twinkled with amusement. But even as she watched, his good humour seemed to die.

"And may we join this horde, if that's the term," said a nearby male voice, "or will you tell me all the seats at this table are taken?"

Dorothea did not need to turn in order to recognize Baskin Haworth, but she looked to see who the *we* included and was not surprised to discover Lord Glissenton accompanying him.

"And if I'm not mistaken," another much less-welcome voice intruded, "I believe you just might have room for two more old friends." Sir Gerald, with Elsa on his arm, gave Dorothea a sardonic smile as they came up behind Amelia. He seemed to be daring her to hint them away.

"Sir Gerald," Miss Oglesby carolled, "you will lend an air of dash and heroism to our little group."

For Dorothea, their presence was all that was needed to set the seal on what must be the most uncomfortable gathering of her experience. And though Amelia had tried to force her into ordering the seating arrangements, it was in fact Lady Ruston who began to place people at the table.

The Duchess of Alverson had outdone herself with succulent dishes prepared for the luncheon. Three courses were followed by almond-paste cups of coffee creams, jellies, tarts, puptons of fruit, trifles and the like. The young people all pronounced it a banquet and looked forward to dinner, which would follow an afternoon of enjoying the gardens and the entertainments Reslon would provide that day.

Dorothea sat at one end of the table with Baskin. Elsa had apparently not given up hopes of Tom, and had attached herself to him, but she was having a singular lack of success. Tom was perfectly polite, but the gushing, enthusiastic boy had somehow disappeared. Sir Gerald had claimed Amelia as his luncheon partner, and they were involved in a discussion so animated that several times the young lady was forced to hide her laughter. Charlie seemed none too pleased to be dividing his attention between Lady Ruston and Miss Oglesby, though the latter was far more interested in talking with Garreth.

"After luncheon, I'm looking forward to having you accompany me through these lovely gardens," Baskin said, but Dorothea shook her head.

"I've a feeling I will be rushing about to keep an eye on my charges," she said. "I cannot pretend to like the company."

"Then doubtless you'll need some assistance," he murmured. "Somehow I don't think you'll get much aid from the quarter you should be able to depend upon."

She wished she could take proper pleasure in his offer, but knowing he had accurately read both her need and Garreth's preoccupation did little to raise her spirits. By the time they had finished their sumptuous repast, it seemed that far more than fate was conspiring against her.

Just as they were rising from the table, Lord Ingleforth appeared at her side.

"Lady Lindsterhope, my profound apologies for intruding," he said, bowing, though his cool eyes seemed to accuse her of defection. "My mother is present, and she desires an introduction." He cast a glance of acute dislike at Baskin, as if expecting him to throw some rub in the way before turning his attention to Dorothea again. "You must know her health does not allow her to come out into society with any regularity."

Dorothea was ready to make her apologies, planning on suggesting a time later in the afternoon, when it would be easier for her to keep an eye on her charges and speak with Lady Ingleforth at the same time, but Lady Ruston, who had been close enough to overhear, stepped into the breach.

"Do allow Lady Amelia and Miss Sailings to walk with us on a turn around the gardens." She gave the group an arch look. "Doubtless they will be well escorted."

Nothing would convince Dorothea that Lady Ruston felt any responsibility toward anything but the establishment of Miss Oglesby, but unable to see a way of refusing to meet Lady Ingleforth, she abjured

Amelia and Farrie to remain in the company of Lady Ruston and allowed Lord Ingleforth to lead her across the lawn to meet his mother.

Lady Ingleforth was an older and more delicate copy of her son, and he had honestly come by his cold eyes, which were never lightened by a smile. For some ten minutes Dorothea conversed with the thin, stiff woman whose compliments held the sickly sweetness of insincerity, and who looked Dorothea over as if she were a possession about to be purchased by the family.

"I do hope you will forgive me for running away," Dorothea said, closing a rather pointed questioning about her family, which had begun to raise her mental bristles. "But I am acting the dragon today, and I must get back to my charges."

"Then I'm sure my son will be happy to escort you." Lady Ingleforth nodded regally.

The last thing Dorothea wanted was the company of the stiff woman's son, but having no way out of it, she accepted his arm and turned in the direction she had seen the luncheon party taking.

One of the garden areas most often described in the guidebooks which mentioned Reslon was termed the Quiet Walkways. They surrounded the maze and were nearly as confusing. The flagstone walks curved in random patterns, shielded on each side by tall hedges and differed from the maze only in that low flowering plants formed colourful verges that gave the strollers a greater sense of openness.

"I daresay you will be quite exhausted if you attempt to seek out the young ladies in that puzzle,"

Lord Ingleforth said, pausing at the entrance to the walks.

"I'm not so paltry, my lord," Dorothea said absently as she listened to the voices that carried through the hedges from the paths beyond. "In any case, as they are my responsibility, if you wish to return to your mother, I won't keep you."

It was obvious by his tightening lips that his lordship had neither the intention of leaving her nor did he plan on entering a search for Farrie and Amelia.

"My dear, I think it would be better if you also return to my mother. I'm sure she would agree I should not allow you to wander in there alone."

It had been too many years since anyone had dictated to her, and even as a schoolgirl she was obstinate when prevented from doing what she considered her duty.

"Sir, since *I* am the only arbitrator of *my* conduct, you needn't fear that you will be blamed for my rash acts."

He reached out as if to stop her, but she eluded his hand and hurried down the path. Fine thing, she thought, if a widow of four and thirty could not walk in a garden alone to find the young ladies she was chaperoning.

But finding them was more of a challenge than she had expected. The gardens of Reslon covered a large acreage, and she was beginning to believe most of it was made up of the Quiet Walkways. She retraced some of her steps several times after hearing voices and laughter which could have been from her party. Her quest might have been easier if she had asked any of the strollers she passed, but to be seen too eagerly seeking Farrie and Amelia could give rise to unwelcome conjecture.

She did not precisely fear for her charges, since she had exacted a promise from them to remain with Lady Ruston; so, though she desired to find them, the matter was not urgent.

A country woman, used to long rambling walks in the woods, she could tell her direction by the shadows, and it seemed to her she had circled behind the maze when around the corner she saw Tom.

"Th-there you are," he said gaily as he came up to her. "Looking for us, I wager. The maze looks like c-capital fun."

"I'm sure it is," Dorothea answered, her eyes on the curving path as she waited for the rest of the party to come into sight. She knew from his stutter that something had occurred to upset him.

"Where are the others?"

"B-back there. I'll show you."

His steps were taking them to the very edge of the hedge-trimmed area, beyond which the eaves of the woods overhung the well-trimmed shrubbery. The voices of the others had faded in the distance when she felt him tense and saw him come to a halt; both movements felt false, as though well rehearsed. He turned to look into a sheltered cove of hedges which partially hid a bench. On it sat Garreth, supporting Miss Oglesby, and though casual passersby might think they had stumbled onto a lovers' tryst, when Garreth saw her his look of profound relief was unmistakable.

"Doro!" Her name exploded from his lips in an enthusiastic burst of sound. "Have you a vinaigrette in your reticule?"

"No, I never carry one," she answered, her own relief evident after that terrible moment of thinking what she saw was a scene of his making. She opened her fan and proceeded to briskly provide what assistance she could. "I suspect the heat and the exertion has overcome her. Tom, do find Lady Ruston."

"I'll be gone only a minute," Tom replied with no trace of his stutter and disappeared down the walk.

Miss Oglesby remained leaning against Garreth for some moments, though the look she gave Dorothea was one of near hatred. Presently she sat up and and announced she was feeling much better. Having seen people genuinely overcome, Dorothea thought her recover was a bit too quickly achieved, though it only pointed out what she suspected.

With her lively imagination, Dorothea could envision the scene which might have followed had Lady Ruston come upon the couple. That Amelia and Farrie, Tom and Charlie would have been unwilling witnesses gave her a strong desire to box the young woman's ears.

"I'm quite all right, and I think we should continue," Miss Oglesby said shortly.

"I think we should remain and wait for your aunt," Dorothea replied, and malice prompted her to add, "since it cannot be thought in any way exceptionable for the three of us to be taking a rest."

Lady Ruston, and the others in train, arrived on the scene before Tom had located them, and Dorothea's suspicions were confirmed. The outraged aunt came striding into the hidden bower, and her assumed shock became real as she saw Dorothea sitting placidly with the young lady. While the others expressed their concern for Miss Oglesby, the matchmaking aunt had time to get her emotions under control, but the gratitude she expressed to Dorothea was barely civil.

"She probably needs rest," Dorothea said. "I'm persuaded she should be taken back to the tents for some cold lemonade. Sir Gerald, I remember you telling us about your ability to keep your direction in confusing terrain on the battlefield. Could we persuade you to lead Miss Oglesby and Lady Ruston back to the pavillions?"

Miss Oglesby had turned an imploring gaze on Garreth, who had regained his composure and was watching the interplay with twinkling eyes, though he remained silent. But thus applied to, Sir Gerald had no recourse but to agree, which he did grudgingly.

As the four walked down the path out the hearing of the rest of the party, Tom rejoined them, and they stood for some minutes before Charlie spoke up.

"Let's go into the maze," he said. "It will be jolly— Amelia and I racing you, Farrie and Glissenton. It's a shame Elsa Palvley went off or we could have had three couples in the contest."

"I'd rather be on my own," Tom said stoutly. "See if I don't beat the rest of you to flinders."

"I think we'd better go along and see to it that they don't tunnel under the hedges," Garreth said to Dorothea as the younger people turned toward the entrance to the maze. When the others were a little ahead he smiled down at her and murmured, "Thank you for coming to Miss Oglesby's aid."

She had been of far more assistance to him than to the young lady, she thought, but perhaps he did believe Miss Oglesby had been ill. If he did, any effort to warn him would make her appear jealous and vindictive.

"I'm sure Lady Ruston will thank me when she's over her concern," she answered crisply, and decided to give him a hint. "But I do wonder that you did not call out to her aunt when Miss Oglesby started feeling unwell."

"We'd fallen a bit behind," he said and seemed to think that called for an explanation. "We were at the rear of the group, because I didn't want the others to straggle since you weren't there to keep an eye on them."

Dorothea bristled at the suggestion that she was shirking her duties.

"I particularly consigned Amelia and Farrie to the care of Lady Ruston," she said sharply. "I wasn't aware your avuncular nature had reasserted itself. You haven't been too attentive of late."

"At least *I'm* not surrounded by a court of suitors," he retorted.

"No matter how large the company, they could always find me," she answered. "That's more than I can say for you since you've taken up with that..." She bit back the last of her remark. Her anger had already betrayed her into saying too much. "This wrangling is serving no useful purpose. It is unnecessary for both of us to enter the maze. Shall you go or shall I?"

"I'll go. *You* can further your friendship with Lady Ingleforth," Garreth snarled.

Since they had by that time reached the entrance to the maze, and the dining tents were in sight, Dorothea turned on her heel and marched off. She had just reached the first tent when Sally Jersey disengaged herself from a group standing in the shade of an awning and approached her.

"Doro, have you seen Garreth?"

"He's with our group of young people," she replied. Sixteen years ago she would have poured out all her woes to her friend, but time had stiffened her pride and insisted she keep her troubles to herself.

"Earlier today I saw that Ruston woman talking to her niece, and they were watching Garreth," Sally said. "I wish you would pay less attention to your suitors and more to keeping that woman from catching him in her snare."

Dorothea could have told Sally the plot they had decided upon had been foiled, but she chose to keep that to herself, also. Sally's mention of her unwanted suitors brought back her sense of ill usage and her anger at Garreth.

"They can have him for all of my concern," she snapped and walked away.

And for at least a minute and a half she meant it.

CHAPTER ELEVEN

GARRETH DECIDED he had spent too much time in the country. Was he getting on in years to the point where he couldn't change his habits? he wondered. No, he wasn't yet infirm, but breakfast just was not appetizing unless he had been out in the early-morning air for a bit of a stroll. The garden at the side of Tolver House was large for a town residence, but used to country life, he still felt confined.

He was making his last turn around the outer perimeter when he heard voices just on the other side of the gate. So low were they that he could not make out the words, but the urgency in the tones convinced him an argument was in progress.

The early hour suggested to him he had nearly intruded on a disagreement between two servants, most likely a romantic contretemps, but as the voices raised slightly he realized both participants were male. Then he recognized Charlie's voice, and after that Tom's; by the stutter which plagued the young baron when he was upset or excited.

Garreth's first inclination was to step through the gate and put an end to the argument before they came to blows. Then he reminded himself that they were young men and should be allowed to handle their problems without interference unless they wanted help. He was turning when he heard Tom's voice raised in exasperation.

"I thought you were my f-friend!"

"A dashed fine one I'd be to let you get in that hobble!" Charlie retorted just as hotly. "Either I'll have your word you'll give it up, or I'll blab the whole thing."

"You *w-wouldn't*!" Outrage caused Tom to speak louder.

"See if I don't!" Charlie answered, nearly at full volume.

Garreth quickened his steps as he approached the gate, opened it and stepped through into the Wilton House garden.

"You'll both blab it to all the servants unless you lower your voices," he said quietly. "Most of the windows are open."

Charlie was seated on a bench sheltered by a yew hedge, his face flushed with the recent argument and looking as embarrassed as if he had been caught in some childish peccadillo. Tom stood stiffly by a flowering peach tree and stared at Garreth as if he had popped up out of the ground. There was no mistaking the fear on the young baron's face, which had turned a sickly white.

"How much d-did...d-did...?" Tom's stutter prevented him from asking his question, but Garreth had heard enough.

"If you mean about the subject of this elevated discussion, nothing."

Relief and colour came into Tom's face again. Charlie opened his mouth to speak and then closed it. He turned a pair of imploring eyes on Tom, but when his silent plea brought no response, his expression hardened.

Garreth took a deep breath. Though he should let them work out their own problems, still there were times when young men in their salad days needed help.

"I'm not going to ask, Tom, but if you've landed yourself in a mess, it's better to come to me than load more problems on Doro. And if you two must continue your argument, take it to a more private place."

Deciding he had said enough, he turned and retraced his steps, going into the breakfast parlour at the back of Tolver House. From the well-laden buffet he had chosen two shirred eggs and a slice of sirloin and was trying to decide between the ham and the herring when the door opened, shuffling footsteps reached his ear and the door closed again.

"The sirloin looks particularly good this morning," he remarked without turning. Since no answer was forthcoming, he made his choice—the ham—and turned back to the table.

Charlie and Tom stood at the side of the room, their faces serious. They made no move toward the sideboard.

"Sit down," Garreth ordered. "I'm not craning my neck to look up at you."

Tom pulled out a chair and sat, turning his head to throw a darkling look at Charlie before he gave his attention to his host.

"I wouldn't be here if I hadn't t-trusted someone I th-thought was my friend," he said mulishly.

"Some people have strange ideas about friends," Charlie muttered, striding around the table and taking a seat on the other side. "*Some* people aren't worth a lead farthing if they try to help, while *some* people are friends even if they land one in a mess by taking one to a place one shouldn't have gone.''

"He's n-not a friend! I know that now!" Tom sputtered angrily and then dropped his eyes to the table.

"I hate to interrupt this philosophical discussion on friendship," Garreth said with the utmost amiability, "but you'd better get to the crux of the matter before James comes in to bring more coffee and toast."

When neither young gentleman took advantage of Garreth's offer, he turned his attention to his plate, saying, "I take it, Tom, you've gotten yourself in a mess. Since Charlie is so ready to talk, why not let him explain it?"

The young men were a few moments communicating by questioning expressions and frowns before Tom shrugged, and Charlie, at first so anxious, began to speak hesitatingly, fingering the empty cup in front of him.

"Tom...Tom... Garreth, why didn't you *tell* us they fuzzed the cards at Madame LeVan's?"

Garreth looked up, his brows raised in surprise. "Because, you young thatchgallows, not being a gamester, I am not much acquainted with the new hells. How much did you lose, Tom?"

Tom opened his mouth, but Charlie overrode him. "Tom didn't go there on his own. He was taken by an ivory-turner he knows—"

"We're not sure he's that bad," Tom interrupted, but Charlie ignored him.

"Well, that's what he turned out to be for all your having known him before. Eric Arnside told us how they get a percentage of the losses when they bring in a flat."

"But I didn't kn-know that!" Tom defended himself hotly against what he saw as an accusation of ignorance. "How could I have known, and him a g-guest at Marvale!"

"All of this is beside the point," Garreth said. "First let's see what it will take to get Tom out of his mess. Then we can assign blame. What's the figure, Tom?"

"Two thousand p-pounds," Tom forced out the figure with a look of anguish, and then went on. "S-sir, I had no idea I was in so deep. H-he said just keep playing and my luck would have to turn. Only it d-didn't."

"And it won't in a place like that," Charlie remarked. Garreth wondered where his ward had picked up that severe tone.

"That's enough, Charlie. Tom, did you really think it would?"

"I didn't know," Tom answered, his misery plain in his voice, but Garreth's lack of anger had helped him to compose himself, and he spoke more clearly. "I never played before because I never liked cards much, and he said . . . But two th-thousand p-pounds!"

"Sir," Charlie broke in breathlessly, "I told him I'd lend him the money and he could pay me back in February when he comes of age, only he wouldn't let me because he knew I'd have to come to you for it. He was going to go to the moneylenders, only I told him if he tried to I'd tell Lady Lindsterhope or you."

"That wouldn't have been your wisest move, Tom," Garreth said quietly to the young baron, who was glaring at Charlie again.

Tom gave his host a hopeless look and fingered the tablecloth. "I know that, sir, but one has to pay one's gambling debts, even if the game was dishonest, and I couldn't go to Doro with it. She and Farrie are making and scraping most of the time, and to tell her I needed... Well, I don't think she has it, and even if she did we'd have to return to Marvale, though save for meeting you and Charlie, I wish we'd stayed there." He shook his head. "I couldn't tell her."

"When did this take place?" Garreth asked him.

"That night you went to Newmarket," Charlie said. "He's been fretting over it ever since. If you'll let me lend him the money, I know he'll pay it back."

Tom's mouth set stubbornly at the idea of accepting it, but his eyes showed his hope that he would be overridden. Garreth decided the time of worry had punished the boy sufficiently.

"As your guardian I can't permit you to do it, Charlie, but I'll lend it to him," Garreth said.

"Sir, it's too much to ask," Tom expostulated, his words at odds with the light in his eyes.

"Unless I mistook the matter, you have far more claim on my help than Charlie's," Garreth replied, which made his ward look curiously from one to the other and Tom to blush.

"Nothing but a trifling thing, sir. No need to feel an obligation. It's I who will be in your debt, and you've no need to worry I'll apply to you a second time. I'm not going near that place—or him—again."

"See," Charlie said triumphantly, "I told you you should have told Garreth!" He had the resiliency of youth, and now that the main problem was solved, he turned his mind to another important issue. He leaned forward and peered at his guardian's plate.

"Is that sirloin as good as it looks?" he enquired.

"Better," Garreth answered as Charlie rose from the table and started for the buffet. "Ring for some more coffee."

Now that his problem was taken care of, Tom was also eyeing his host's plate and the well-laden sideboard.

"Do you think there's any tea, sir? To tell you the truth, I've not had much appetite lately, but that beef does look good."

"Oh, Lord," Garreth groaned. "Charlie, order up another whole cow, and you two can't have all the sweet rolls, so don't think it."

DOROTHEA WAS CONVINCED Garreth had no inkling of the intent of Miss Oglesby and Lady Ruston when the young lady feigned her illness in the garden at Reslon. She was sure that no man who understood such a blatant, treacherous attempt to snare him in a matrimonial trap could continue to give a female the attention he lavished on Miss Oglesby.

Though his and Dorothea's disagreement that afternoon had been sharp, they had ignored it thereafter, and there had been no change in their friendship. It was becoming increasingly hard for her to see him so often with a growing conviction that their relationship would never reach beyond where it stood when they were hardly more than children.

She could not have stood it if she had not had other concerns. Lord Glissenton's constant attendance was only a minor irritation beside the constant and flagrant attention Sir Gerald was giving Amelia. Amelia did not seem to favour him above anyone else, and indeed became sharp with him when his flirtation approached impropriety, but when Farrie tried to warn the earl's daughter of the adventurer, Amelia had become quite sharp with her.

The afternoon at Reslon had freed Dorothea of two pressing problems. Lord Ingleforth had become so incensed over her refusal to allow him to dictate to her that he had immediately begun to pursue another lady of reputed means. Dorothea wished him good fortune. And since the Prince Regent had decided to retire to Brighton because of the unseasonable heat, Mr. Cheyney was no longer in town.

They were three days away from the Wilton House ball, and while the house was being turned out, one had to take care to keep from falling over rolled-up carpets, maids industriously polishing the chair legs, and other such impediments to free movement. Mrs. Hicks had assured her that the champagne, the newly covered tables for the card room, and scores of similar needs had been delivered and were in readiness, and that she had an extra pastry chef as well as extra servants coming in to prepare the food. Used to a mistress who took no interest in details, Mrs. Hicks had made her arrangements with Amelia's assistance, and after talking with the housekeeper, Dorothea had no doubt the ball would go off without a hitch.

In addition, the morning's post had brought a letter from Lady Harriet, informing Dorothea that she would be arriving in town shortly, though what that might mean, she had no idea. It was enough that Amelia's mother would be there to put a stop to Sir Gerald's attempts to fix her daughter's interest.

Dorothea was just folding the letter when Tom came into the breakfast parlour. "Good morning, sweet Doro," he said gaily as he headed for the buffet. "You look in fine fettle this morning."

"A missive from Lady Harriet and Lord Wilton informs me they are on their way to London," she said. "I'm freed of a worry. I was persuaded they would not be able to return, and I would have to act as hostess for the ball."

"Glad they're coming back. I hope Lord Wilton will send Sir Gerald packing," Tom said. "I'll tell you, I don't like his attentions to Amelia."

Dorothea looked up, startled to hear him speak out against the man who had been his idol only a few weeks previously. When Tom saw her confusion, he coloured and turned away to fill his plate before coming back to take his seat at the table.

"I suppose I should tell you," he said slowly. "I've learned something about him you might not know." Haltingly he told her about meeting Sir Gerald the night he had supposedly gone with Charlie and the Arnside gentlemen to Cribb's Parlour, and had accompanied the ex-cavalry officer to a gambling hell. He confessed his losses, and before she had time to take in the full meaning of it, he assured her he had arranged a loan from Garreth.

"I couldn't tell you, knowing how you'd scrimped and saved, and what that much money would have meant to us," he said. "I kept thinking back to what a fortune that seemed a year ago, even now."

Dorothea tried to calm the sinking feeling with rationale. Two thousand pounds would not seem so much when Tom was in control of his fortune, and it certainly seemed that he had learned a lesson.

"I can't understand how I could have done it," he said miserably.

"Doubtless a few glasses of wine made the amounts seem far less than what they totalled out to be," she said.

"Champagne," he confirmed. "And to tell you the truth, I don't care for it above half, or cards, either."

Since Amelia and Farrie entered the room at that moment the disclosures came to a halt. Amelia had also received a letter from her mother, and spent part of the morning discussing with the housekeeper the menu for the upcoming ball.

Tom and Farrie joined Charlie for a ride in the park, and because the day had already begun to warm, Dorothea decided to walk in the garden before the temperature rose enough to take the freshness from the air. Walking helped her think, and she found herself in need of preparing a speech of gratitude to Garreth for rescuing Tom from his troubles. She also wanted to add Tom's assurances that the loan would be repaid as soon as the trust was ended.

At noon she was still trying to form in her mind the words to express her gratitude when two heavily laden coaches drew up in front of the house, signalling the arrival of Lady Harriet and Lord Wilton.

"Terrible day for travelling. Glad to see that girl of ours hasn't burned down the house. Someone get me a large pot of tea,'' Lady Harriet announced as she strode into the hall, tossing her bonnet at the butler, her gloves at a footman and striding on toward the steps to the first floor with Dorothea following helplessly in her wake.

"Is Lady Cynthia's health improved?" Dorothea asked.

"As dear as my great-aunt is to me, her crotchets will have to wait until after we've done our duty by Amelia,'' she said forthrightly. "Doubtless I'll have to return to Salvermain after the ball, but I could not remain there when my duty is to my girl.''

Outside the house Lord Wilton was shouting for the footmen and anyone else who could carry in the trunks and portmanteaux. The two ladies were halfway up the steps when his lordship strode in shouting orders and leading a train of overburdened servants.

He followed the ladies into the drawing room where even through the closed door they could hear the sounds of luggage being carried in. He paused only long enough to pour a glass of port from a tray of decanters and glasses which had been set ready. Then he dropped into a tub chair. As soon as he was seated, Lady Harriet came straight to the point.

"Out with it, Lady Lindsterhope. What's that girl of ours been up to while we were away?"

Dorothea had admonished herself not to be shocked at the bluntness of the Easterlys, but she was still taken aback.

"No shilly-shallying, mind,'' the earl said. "We know that naughty little puss, and we won't hold you responsible for her starts.''

"But she hasn't done the least thing," Dorothea objected. "I can't say I'm overly fond of all the gentlemen who have tried to attach themselves to her, but she can hardly be faulted for either her beauty or your circumstances drawing their attention. I don't think she's to blame. She has not been flirting."

"Nonsense, all pretty chits flirt," Lord Wilton said. "Can't expect her not to take some advantage of her looks."

"Fortune-hunters buzzing around her?" Lady Harriet nodded. "Would be, I suppose. Who?"

Dorothea could have wished herself anywhere else, but since she was anxious to rid herself of her worries, she felt she had to speak.

"Sir Gerald Palvley has been a bit too attentive for my peace."

"Don't know him," Lord Wilton said.

"I cannot say more than it is not a connection I would have for Farrie," Dorothea said. "We hinted him away from her while we were still at Marvale."

"Look into it," Lord Wilton said with no more urgency than if he were considering the purchase of a horse. Still, she had no doubts that within a week he would know far more about Sir Gerald than she did. "Anyone else need hinting away?"

"There's Lord Glissenton." Dorothea paused, because there was certainly nothing she could say against the young gentleman. "I know that's not a connection you would approve of, Lady Harriet, since I heard you warn Lady Amelia about him the night we met."

Lord Wilton had been frowning as she mentioned the second of Amelia's beaux, and he turned his disapproval on his wife.

"Is she talking about Boater Glissenton's boy? What the deuce could you have against him? One of the best families in the country, and one of the warmest, if they haven't hit hard times." He laughed heartily. "No chance old Boater would gamble away his fortune."

"Boater and Bess Glissenton were two of the dullest sticks in the country when they were young," Lady Harriet said.

"Can't even figure how Amelia would meet him, much less attract his attention," Lord Wilton mused.

"I saw to it," Lady Harriet said, her chin coming up. "Amelia was ripe for a scrape, upset over that Kettling chit snubbing Charlie. I didn't think she'd come to any harm with a stuffy sort like Glissenton. If he was raised by Bess, he'd keep to the line. But can you see Amelia in that family? She'd be bored enough to be kicking up a lark within a month. Never do."

"No, suppose it wouldn't," he said and then turned back to Dorothea. "No scrapes, no schemes, no larks, huh? She's been easy on you, but we'd better keep an eye on her. Been too good too long." His smile was that of a proud father. "Mark you, she's up to *something*."

During the weeks Lady Harriet and Lord Wilton had been out of town, Wilton House had run with silent, unseen efficiency, but once the mistress returned, her orders for the ball threw most of the servants into a frenzy of activity, though it soon became apparent to Dorothea that the confusion only

lasted until Lady Harriet was out of the room and
Mrs. Hicks took charge again.

Still, Dorothea found herself often seeking refuge
in the garden during the next three days. She was
seated on a bench by the wall on the afternoon of
Amelia's ball when she chanced to see Garreth coming through the gate.

Since the return of the Easterlys she had not had an
occasion to speak privately with him and so had not
yet thanked him for helping Tom. Thinking she had
the opportunity, she called to him and he came to join
her on the bench.

"Hiding from the mêlée inside, I see," he said. "I
wouldn't come within a mile of the place if I didn't
want to make sure the flowers had been delivered."

"They did arrive and they're beautiful," Dorothea
said. "Is it customary to send corsages to all the ladies in the house on the night of a ball? I don't remember ever seeing it done. Amelia, Farrie and I
thank you, and Charlie, and Tom. We'll certainly have
a hard decision between three bouquets."

"Since we didn't know what would suit, we went
together and picked out three different colours,"
Garreth admitted. "I just hope Charlie's were right for
Amelia. She'll want to wear his."

Dorothea was silent and he took that for a hesitation.

"I know she'll get flowers from all her beaux, but
the ones from an old friend are safest," he said. "Believe me, she'll take the safest course when push comes
to shove."

"I wasn't thinking of Amelia's flowers," Dorothea
admitted. "For days I've been rehearsing a speech and

now that I have a chance to talk with you alone, I'm afraid it's gone clean out of my head.''

"Something desperate?" he asked, a puzzled smile lighting his face.

"Desperate gratitude," she said. "Tom told me about his gambling losses. I confess I cannot understand his allowing himself to lose so much money. Since I cannot even assist him in paying it back until the trust is ended, I can only thank you and promise that you will be paid."

"The young cawker should have kept his mouth shut," he said with a trace of irritation. "And the debt is between him and me."

"But so much!" She was still astounded by the amount.

"Cheap at the price," he said. "I wouldn't worry if I were you."

"Two thousand pounds might be cheap to you—" she started to object, but Garreth cut her off.

"But it's wealth to Tom," he said. "That's why it's better that he lost a lot than just a little. People who lose their entire fortunes do it a little at a time in the beginning. His loss was too much too soon. I expect he's cured of gambling."

"I suppose you're right, and you can't know what a relief it is to think of his experience in that light. I have to thank you again for easing my mind." She smiled up at him. "I suppose you'll be glad when the season is over and we return to Marvale. We have certainly been a trial to you."

She was gathering her sewing, and Garreth rose, offering her his hand as she prepared to stand. When he spoke his voice was low and distant.

"Have you heard me complain, Doro?"

"You're far too much of a gentleman for that," she said.

"Will you always refuse to know me, Doro? Will you always refuse to see that I may have my own reasons?"

He bowed and turned to pass through the gate and into his own garden, leaving her looking after him and wondering what he could possibly mean.

CHAPTER TWELVE

As HE WAS NEW TO SOCIETY, Charlie had no idea what he had done that first night at Almack's. Reacting to Miss Kettling's snubbing, he had meant only to hide his embarrassment by giving his attention to the Misses Duval and their female friends, the number of which seemed to grow with every social occasion.

The mothers of these less-pulchritudinous young ladies, who had not let parental affection blind them to their daughters' physical shortcomings, had watched with increasing wonder and gratification as their daughters received the attentions of a young marquess, and the equally handsome Baron of Lindsterhope. In short order, Lord Farling and the dandified but wealthy Mr. Nelson arrived on the scene, and soon to follow came the highly respected Arnside gentlemen and several of their friends. True, most of these young blades of society were as yet too young to be thinking of marriage, and did pass the line in leading the young ladies to unseemly laughter or to move about the floor with more enthusiasm than necessary.

Still, not one hopeful mama was willing to draw her daughter away from the group, particularly Lady Duval, because it had led to her eldest daughter, Ellie, whose height was the despair of the family, meeting the tall, gangly, but exquisitely wealthy and eligible

Mr. Franklin-Wate. Mr. Richard Arnside, the eldest
of the five brothers who were reputed to be the leaders of a quiet, respectable set of young men about
town, was paying particular attention to the younger
Miss Sarah Duval. Yet in her complacency, Lady Duval could not help but wonder what had happened to
Lords Ridgeley and Lindsterhope, because they were
inexplicably absent from the group and had been for
some time. Since this particular ball was at Wilton
House, where the Sailings were guests, and the marquess was reputed to be a close friend of Lady Amelia's, it did seem strange.

Lady Duval would have thought it still more odd if
she had been privy to a low-voiced conversation which
had taken place nearly an hour earlier.

Charlie had paid little attention when one of the
footmen had approached Tom and had given him a
message in a voice too low to be overheard. He'd
thought it a bit strange when Tom had disappeared
through one of the tall windows opening onto the terrace. He was well aware of the trap Lady Ruston and
her niece had attempted to spring on Garreth, and
when Charlie had recovered from the shock of it, he
had found his sense of self-preservation considerably
heightened.

Tom's sudden trip to the terrace looked havey-
cavey, and he decided to have a look-see. But another
guest had seen Tom's exit from the room. Farrie de-
tached herself from a group of young ladies and took
Charlie's arm as he started toward the partially opened
window drapery. A good thing, he thought, since a
female on the scene would lend countenance to a tête-
à-tête if some chit was trying a scheme on his friend,

and Tom would be there to chaperon Farrie. It did pass all bounds that Sir Gerald and his sister had arrived at Amelia's ball, but short of creating a scene there was little any of them could do.

When Charlie and Farrie stepped out onto the terrace they were surprised to find Tom in hurried conversation with his groom. The marquess was so relieved he strolled up grinning.

"Going for a trot through the park at this hour?" Charlie remarked, then let the rest of his banter die. His first thought, that trouble was afoot, was verified by the expression on his friend's face.

"What's amiss?"

"Sir Gerald's carriage is waiting in the laneway," Tom said.

"He's after Amelia!" Charlie announced, turning toward the door as if to rush into the ballroom, but Farrie caught his arm.

"No, she wouldn't be so foolish," she said, trying to bring some order to the conversation.

"It's just the cod-headed sort of thing she might do," Charlie disagreed. "Not withstanding her ball, she's getting devilish bored with all this social to-do."

"But he wouldn't w-want Amelia," Tom objected. "She ain't mistress of her own money yet."

"He's likely counting on Lord Wilton handing over the dibs to set them up in style once the knot is tied," said a quiet voice behind them. They whirled to see Lord Glissenton step out of the shadows. When the new arrival saw their alarm he smiled. "I'm a little familiar with Sir Gerald, and I'd put nothing past the man, particularly tonight. He's looking as smug as a cat over a creampot."

"He danced with Amelia earlier," Farrie told them.

"That's right, and they were talking in a dashed cosy way I didn't like at all," Charlie said darkly. "There's something afoot, and I'm going to get it out of her if I have to shake her."

"You'll only put her back up," Tom warned.

"The domino!" Farrie said, her eyes widening. "I saw her shaking out her domino this evening when I went into her room before dinner!"

"She's planning to elope for sure," Tom said, shifting his feet as if he were ready for action and needed a plan to put his energy into motion.

"Someone's going to elope, but it ain't going to be Amelia," Charlie said, suddenly grinning. "Farrie, didn't you and Amelia plan some rig on us for the Hamilton masquerade?"

"How did you know about that?" she demanded. "And I don't see— Oh! You mean both of us getting pink dominoes!"

"G-good Lord, this is not time to be talking about f-frills and f-finery," Tom stuttered in exasperation.

"Finery is just exactly what we need," Charlie said, still grinning from ear to ear. "We're going to make Sir Gerald a bride."

Lord Glissenton raised his eyebrows and looked at the marquess warily. "What do you have in mind?"

"We're going to let Sir Gerald elope with a wealthy bride," Charlie said, grinning. "We'll give him Tom."

"What!" Tom ejaculated.

"Can't you see his face when he discovers Tom in the carriage?"

"W-well, he won't!" Tom retorted.

"It can't possibly work," Glissenton said, a chuckle in his voice. "But, oh Lord, if it could, that would be a good one."

"But it can with all of us to pull it off," Charlie said. "He can't just walk out of the ballroom with Amelia. He will have to meet her in the garden, and the only way she can get out of the house in a domino is through the garden door on the ground floor."

"I'm not dressing up in women's clothes," Tom said. "Wouldn't I look a cake, and I wouldn't put it past him to put a bullet in me when he finds out."

"He won't, because Glissenton and I will follow right behind. You don't think we'd miss the fun, do you?"

"I'm still not wearing women's clothes," Tom insisted.

"You wouldn't have to actually wear them," Farrie said, her eyes shining. "I know just how to do it. You won't have to put on a dress, Tom."

"I don't like this," Tom asserted, but a slow smile crossed his face. "But think of how he'll look." He gave a crack of laughter. "No one will have a better view of it than I will. It's almost worth taking a bullet . . . You'll be there?" he asked Charlie anxiously.

Charlie nodded, and Glissenton added, "And so will I. I don't believe it will work, and if someone doesn't get shot we'll likely be taken up by the watch, but I wouldn't miss it."

"Right," Charlie said. "Here's what we're going to do. You, Glissenton, stay with Amelia until Farrie gets the domino and whatever else Tom needs. Then, Farrie, you're to stick close to Amelia, and Glissenton and I will be on the lookout. . . ."

Before Charlie's plan could be put into action, he had to overcome Tom's, Lord Glissenton's and Farrie's objections, and his patience was wearing thin before he had spelled out every step and they left him to do their parts.

Charlie's plan called for him to go down into the garden and watch the gate leading to the laneway by the side of the stables. A light mist hung in the air, but the night was not precisely chilly, so he was tolerably comfortable for the half hour it took Farrie to gather the clothing with which she disguised Tom.

Then Lord Glissenton appeared, strolling along the path as if he were just out blowing a smoke. Charlie tapped him on the arm and drew him into the shadow of a small, vine-covered arbour that sheltered a bench and two chairs.

"This is all very well, but Palvley is still in the ballroom," Glissenton said. "And what if he tries to leave the house by the ground-floor door?"

"Don't think he can, but tell you what," Charlie said. "You keep watch here for a bit, and I'll keep an eye on him inside. It won't do for any of us to be gone too long at a time."

Suiting action to words, Charlie hurried back up the stone steps leading to the terrace and paused to take a deep breath before entering the ballroom. The Wiltons might be country folk, but both the lord and his lady had been well-known when they were on the social scene, and it seemed they had drawn society en masse for Amelia's ball.

"Lord, what a crush," Charlie muttered and searched the crowd for Sir Gerald. He made a complete circuit of the ballroom, and the crowd had begun to thin as the guests went in to supper. A quick look round those gathered at the buffet and the tables elicited no sight of his quarry. He was hurrying back toward the card room when he was accosted by Lady Kettling, walking with her daughter.

"Lord Ridgeley," the older woman chirruped as if she had seen a long-lost acquaintance. "How delightful, and here we are, by some odd circumstance, without a gentleman to take us in to supper."

Charlie would not have been human if, after his snubbing by Miss Kettling, he had not entertained a vision of just such a thing happening. Days before he had even seen himself giving in with obvious reluctance and forcing the young lady to be charming to win him over. That his dream could actually come true and at this time, was not only startling, but vexing.

"Delighted to be of assistance, but . . ." Lord, what could he say? "Got a rock in my shoe!" he announced desperately and reinforced the statement by limping a step or two.

"You've what?" Mr. Haworth appeared behind the ladies just in time to hear Charlie's excuse, and looked as if he would laugh.

"Got a rock in my shoe," Charlie repeated, and then wondered how he could explain it since there were no stones on the pavement between Tolver and Wilton House.

"More likely a shirt stud or a watch fob. Mr. Haworth will be glad to lead you in," he said, hobbling off. "Matter of fact it feels like it could be the whole watch and chain," he said, trying to add veracity to his story. He had rounded the corner before he discovered he was now limping on the right foot when he'd begun on the left.

He was intensely relieved to discover Sir Gerald in the card room in discussion with Lord Carmly, and moving closer, he was even gladder he had followed the rogue.

"Just a touch of the headache," Sir Gerald was saying. "I'm engaged to sup with Miss Varrington, but afterward I'll be taking my leave, so if Lady Carmly would not mind escorting Elsa home..."

Charlie congratulated himself and hurried out of the room, then down the hall past the supper room, casting one anxious eye on the succulent-looking lobster patties. Ten to one the Arnsides would scoff the lot before he could get back. Amelia deserved a good shaking, he decided.

Then he saw Amelia, leading Lady Ruston toward the door, talking animatedly to her.

Now what was that chit up to? But he didn't dare ask. One hint that he knew about the elopement and she might rush right out to Sir Gerald's carriage before he could stop her. But whatever she was about, he would put a spoke in her wheel when she came out the garden door. He hurried back through the ballroom, out onto the terrace and down the steps, his first destination the arbour to warn Glissenton. Then he stepped inside the garden door and into the boot room on the right, where Tom was muttering about his disguise.

"Ha, if you don't look a sight," Charlie said with a laugh, but before Tom could give him more than a fulminating look, he had his friend by the arm. "It won't be long now. I heard Palvley making his excuses, and Amelia is definitely up to something."

"The horses saddled?" Tom asked as he lifted the hem of the full domino to keep from tripping over it as he followed Charlie out of the house and into the shade of the arbour.

"All ready," Charlie assured him. "I don't think he'll go far before he finds out, and when he does all you have to do is drop that handkerchief out the window, and we'll see it fall."

"Speaking of handkerchiefs, I'd better get over there and do my part, since I'm in this," Glissenton said. He hurried across the garden to take his place behind a tall shrub.

"What if he speaks to me?" Tom whispered. "I can't answer, I don't sound like Amelia."

"He won't before he gets you in the carriage," Charlie assured him. "He won't risk the stable boys hearing him, so he'll be quiet."

"Look!" Tom pointed across the garden to where Glissenton was waving a white handkerchief. By its closeness to the ground he was signalling the presence of someone on the terrace.

The two young lords stood quietly as Sir Gerald, making his way toward the stable, hurried down the steps from the terrace and along the garden path and out of sight behind the tall shrubbery.

Several minutes passed and Glissenton waved again, and this time the handkerchief was higher. If everything was going according to plan, Farrie had stepped to the window of the ballroom and pulled the draperies back a fraction, indicating that Amelia had disappeared from the festivities.

Not much later they heard the squeak of the garden door and light footsteps on the walk. Charlie reached out to grab the arm of the lady in the domino who was just passing the arbour, but to his surprise, he found himself pushed, and he nearly lost his balance.

The caped and hooded figure hurried on down the path while Charlie's assailant held one small but strong hand over his mouth and gripped his arm fiercely.

He was staring down into Amelia's eyes and they were full of anger.

DOROTHEA HAD ALSO WONDERED what Amelia was doing in the company of Lady Ruston when she had seen the two of them leave the supper room, but in the perversity of her mood she came up with an answer: doubtless Garreth had made his partiality known to his good friends the Earl and Countess of Wilton, and the entire family felt it behooved them to accept his future wife.

During supper she had taken a glass of lemonade, but had no appetite for any of the succulent dishes prepared for the guests. After making sure Farrie was in a group being watched over by an eagle-eyed mama, she wandered back into the nearly empty ballroom, stepped through the draperies and strolled up the terrace toward the front of the house, hoping the air would cool her and help to lighten her mood.

She heard the booted footsteps of a gentleman leaving the ballroom, but caught up in her own misery, she did not turn to see who had come out to take the air. In any case the stroller had turned in the other direction and had taken the steps down to the garden. She paced back and forth for some minutes, and decided that not even a long walk among the bluebells of Marvale could have raised her blighted spirits. She had started back toward the French doors leading out of the ballroom when Sir Gerald stepped out onto the terrace.

Not wanting to meet him, she turned and hurried in the other direction, trying the doors that led into a small sitting room closer to the front of the house. Luckily they were open. She stepped into the room with a feeling of intense relief.

The music had begun again, and knowing her duty, she crossed the room and walked up the hall to the ballroom, determined to do right by Farrie, though it seemed to her that the entire season had become a misery and she heartily wished she had never left Marvale.

Mr. Haworth was just leaving the ballroom, and when he saw her, he quickened his steps.

"Doro, I've been looking for you," he said, and she thought there was some nervousness in his attitude. "Tell me, that room you just stepped out of. Is it empty?"

"Why, yes," she answered, wondering at the reason for his question.

"Then let us step in there. What I want to say to you is of a private nature."

"But Farrie..." She tried to object, but he firmly turned her around and started back down the hall.

"She's with Lady Wilton, who was, when I last saw them, introducing her to a singularly handsome young man. She can do without you for a bit."

By that time he had led her into the small sitting
room and then to a chair. With his guidance she sat,
looking at him expectantly. It was in her mind that he
was going to tell her something about Tom, and she
felt her pulse thudding dully against her temples. Tom
had managed to get himself into another scrape, she
thought, and while she dreaded to hear what it was,
she was glad he'd had the good sense to turn to her
cousin.

With her mind on her wards it was not surprising
that when Mr. Haworth took a seat across from her
and puffed himself up to speak, she did not at first
take his meaning.

"I hope my sitting doesn't offend you, Doro. I'd
feel a fool on my knees."

"I...don't...?" She stared at him as if he had lost
his senses.

"Doro." He leaned forward and took her hand, a
soft smile lighting his face. "You must know I have
been fond of you ever since we played our first game
of jackstraws. I don't know if it will weigh with you,
but after your father's death, your brother, James,
had it in mind to make a match between us."

The realization that he was making her an offer hit
her with a blinding wonderment, and after a gasp she
struggled for an answer that was only a sparring for
time while she gathered her wits.

"I take it you didn't come up to scratch, as the saying goes?" She tried to keep her voice light, but heard
the crack in it.

"I wasn't told. My father thought me too young and
put a stop to it by refusing the settlement. That's what

James was after, of course. If they'd put it to me your life might have been quite different, and mine, too."

"Your father was wise," she said softly. "I'm no longer of a mind that fondness is enough on which to base a marriage. Silly of me to be romantic, but there it is." She hoped she had not injured his dignity, but better a small hurt now than a life of misery.

"I agree with you," he said, gently patting the hand he held. "I assure you these past few days I've found my feelings steadily deepening into love. And while I don't pretend that we've had the time to develop a deep relationship, will you give us that time and chance, Doro?"

She gazed into his eyes and saw a man who would spend his life trying to make her happy. Farrie liked him, Tom both liked and respected him, and Baskin Haworth had already shown himself to be a man of the world who could help a young inexperienced sprig find his way in society.

She had always kept a little piece of her heart for Baskin, but not her whole heart. That belonged to Garreth, and Baskin deserved better.

"I would that I could say yes," she said slowly, "but I'm afraid I could never return your affection—not the way you offer it." She dropped her gaze to the hand he still held, not wanting to see his expression.

After a moment he spoke again, his voice soft, caressing. "You don't think you could learn to love me if you tried, Doro?"

Not trusting her voice or wanting to meet his gaze, she kept her head lowered as she shook it slowly.

"I won't stop trying," he said, "unless you tell me there is another who already has a claim on your affection."

She took a deep breath. "I'm afraid you have guessed the reason, but since you have, you must know I could not in good conscience accept your offer."

"It's Garreth, isn't it?"

Despite her efforts, she felt the tears gathering behind her lashes and withdrew her hand to search in her reticule for her handkerchief.

"There's never been anyone but Garreth," she admitted. "After all these years, I cannot see myself altering now."

"Poor Doro." Mr. Haworth took her hand again and patted it gently.

Then suddenly she felt his hands quiet and stiffen as if the sympathy had been withdrawn or pulled away by another emotion. She looked up and froze.

Garreth was standing in the doorway.

CHAPTER THIRTEEN

To Dorothea, it seemed as if the tableau would never come to an end. She and Baskin sat in two facing chairs by the hearth where the fire had been not yet been lit, and Garreth stood in the doorway, one hand carelessly on the velvet draperies that hid the frame. For what seemed like an age, but could have been only a moment or so, they were frozen in position, held by Garreth's overhearing her admission.

Then Garreth let the drapery drop and slowly strolled into the room. When he spoke his voice held an amiability at odds with his words.

"Would you mind getting out, old man?" he said to Baskin.

Dorothea clutched her cousin's fingers as if to stop him, but he gently disengaged his hand and rose.

"I think it's about time," he said, and quitted the room.

When he was gone, Garreth came forward as if to take the chair Baskin had vacated, but to forestall him Dorothea jumped up and walked to the window. She was still holding the handkerchief she had pulled from her reticule, and she twisted it with nervous fingers.

"I can't think what made me say that," she said, trying a laugh, which came out as a brittle twitter.

"One must say something when one wants to turn away a suitor, and I'm sure you will understand it was the likeliest thing to send him on his way." She knew she was babbling, but anything was better than what she supposed must be his reaction to what he had overheard.

"Is that why you said it, Doro?"

She thought Baskin had used caressing tones, but Garreth's voice seemed to enfold her in a sensuous wrapping.

"Of course. We friends are here to help each other out of our scrapes, after all. I hope you will do the same if you ever find yourself in such a situation, and don't think I would ever hold you to anything you found need to say, as I know you won't blame me or hold me to it."

Not that he would, she thought, after the attention he had been paying to Miss Oglesby.

"You give me too much credit, my dear."

"Then you would never need such recourse, since a gentleman has the option of making an offer, but you can see that I was in a hobble," she said as she worked her way round a chair, hoping to circle him slowly before he knew what she was up to and thereby make a rush for the door and the safety of the crowded ballroom. Anything was better than turning to face him.

"But I'm in a predicament as far as offers go," he said softly, and to her dismay she saw his shadow on the wall as he moved, cutting off her escape. "You see, sixteen years ago I made an offer, and until I receive an answer, I find myself caught."

He moved closer, and suddenly she felt his hands rest lightly on her shoulders.

"I do think if a lady has kept me waiting sixteen years for an answer it would be unconscionable for her to refuse me."

"Oh, but that wasn't a real offer—just help from a friend," Dorothea said breathlessly, desperately wanting him to deny it. "And I didn't know about it until my brother's death five years later, honestly I did not."

"I doubt aging helped it any, and I admit I could have been awkward, not having made a proposal of marriage before," he said, slowly turning her to face him. "And I doubt I'll do much better now. I haven't made one since, you know."

He was gazing down at her with a soft half-smile which sent her pounding pulse into a gallop.

"But . . . Miss Oglesby," she said. "I thought you were fixing her interest."

He grinned. "I'm not the first one to set up a flirt when his attention to the woman in his life was causing talk. And I couldn't let her pull her tricks on young Gresham. His father was a friend of mine."

"What if she tries again?"

"Too late, the *Gazette* will carry the announcement of the Gresham-Edwards betrothal tomorrow morning, and the rest of the world can take care of itself from now on."

"Oh," she murmured, and ducking her head, she stepped closer, burying her face against his lapel. "I couldn't believe you could feel any partiality for me with all the younger ladies present."

To herself she seemed to have approached the line of being wanton in inviting his embrace by moving closer. Then to her momentary but intense embarrassment, he tightened his hold on her shoulders and stepped back, but she soon saw it was to look down at her face. His expression seemed to suggest she had lost her wits.

"Good God, Doro, after years of having a group of halflings around, do you think I'd want to marry one? Make sense woman. You're far more to my style than any of them could be!" He paused, pulled her to him in the embrace she had been seeking, and took a deep breath. When he spoke again his voice was hoarse. "Besides, you silly chit, I love you. You'd have known it before if you hadn't been making light of me every time I brought up that letter."

"But I never believed—"

She didn't get to finish her statement because he raised her chin. "Woman, when will you learn not to talk so much?"

He allowed her no chance to object as his lips came down on hers and proved beyond any doubt that his feelings were not that of a youngster offering help to a friend.

She was still standing in his embrace when rapid footsteps on the terrace approached the open French doors and warned them of an imminent interruption.

"There won't be anyone in here," Amelia was saying breathlessly, and a moment later the draperies were flung aside and she entered, followed by Charlie and Tom.

Dorothea and Garreth stared as they saw the young baron, still dressed in the pink domino, and through the opening in the cape they caught sight of a satin underslip.

"Tom!" Dorothea gasped, torn between shock and laughter.

"Lord, what have you wretched brats been up to now?" Garreth demanded.

"S-someone help me out of this," Tom muttered, trying to untie the strings of the domino and making a botch of it in his haste.

Dorothea hurried over to help him as he jerked at the ties, knotting them tighter. "Tom this is going far, too far beyond the line. What if a guest walked in and saw you dressed like this?" The vision of Sally's face if she chanced to come in was a horror. She forced the image from her mind and turned to helping her embarrassed ward, whose expression had darkened at the censure.

"W-wasn't my idea, and the d-dashed strings wouldn't untie in the dark," he muttered.

"What have you been doing?" Garreth demanded again.

"Oh, Uncle Garreth, it's been the most perfect rig," Amelia said as she also helped Tom, her nimble fingers working at a second set of ties. "Will you hold still, you silly thing?"

"Doro's messing up my neckcloth," Tom complained.

"Of course these two and Lord Glissenton nearly ruined everything," Amelia said, her glance flickering toward Garreth as she ignored Tom's complaint.

"I like that," Charlie retorted. "We were only trying to save your bacon."

"Much it needed saving." Amelia tossed her head. "I laid my plans, and even if they hadn't gone off as I expected, I wouldn't have been in any danger."

"Cut line and tell me what you've been up to, or I'll call in John," Garreth threatened, but Amelia gave him a wicked smile.

"Papa will just laugh and tell me I'm the bane of his peace."

"She was going to elope with Sir Gerald," Charlie said, coming to the crux of the matter.

"Only she wasn't—it was a rig," Tom hastily added, sounding relieved now that Amelia and Doro had finished untying the strings of the domino. When it dropped to the floor it revealed a white satin underskirt tied to his waist with a ribbon and hanging in front like an apron.

"And obviously you were part of it," Garreth said, not as much upset by what he was hearing as Dorothea was, who felt as if she might swoon with shock.

"You see, we were going to let Tom elope in her place," Charlie explained as if it were the most natural thing in the world. "But Amelia had a better idea." He gave her another hot look. "But she could have let us in on it."

Just at that moment the drapery that covered the door into the hallway was pulled aside and Farrie entered, her face alight with laughter. Close on her heels was Lord Glissenton. Since they seemed taken aback to find Dorothea and Garreth present but neither looked at all surprised to see Tom's condition, it was easy to suppose they were also involved in the adventure.

"Well, my idea was better than yours, and I didn't need any help or anyone to create confusion or give it away with a loose tongue," Amelia said, ignoring the new arrivals. "There was nothing for it—Sir Gerald's making a cake of himself and me, trying to get his hands on Papa's fortune—but to finally tell him I'd elope with him tonight after supper if he brought his carriage around to the lane."

"Only Jarvis suspected something was going forward, so he came and told me the carriage was there," Tom cut in. "He recognized those rawboned steppers of Sir Gerald's, and since he saw baggage strapped on behind, he was worried that the rogue was up to something."

"No one leaves their carriage in a back lane with portmanteaux strapped to the back when just coming to a ball," Charlie said with all the experience of several weeks in society.

"If you knew this, why didn't you come and tell me?" Garreth demanded. "I'd have made short shift of him soon enough."

"Because you and Papa would have been so outraged we would have had a scandal," Amelia said. "And I've no intention to be the object of gossip. I must say, even Charlie had a better notion than that."

"Well, I thought so, too," Charlie said, mollified by the faint praise. "We were going to kidnap Amelia when she started down the path in the garden and put Tom in her place. Then Glissenton and I were going to jump on our horses and ride after the carriage. We wanted to be in on the fun when Sir Gerald found out he had Tom instead of Amelia. And to bring Tom back, of course." This last sounded as if it were an afterthought.

"I must remember to start carrying a vinaigrette," Dorothea murmured as she took a chair and watched while Amelia freed Tom of the satin petticoat.

"But Amelia's idea was even better," Charlie said. "She never planned to go."

"I can't wait to hear it." Garreth turned to Amelia.

"I sent Miss Oglesby in my place."

"You what?" Dorothea asked weakly.

"We knew what she tried to do to you, Uncle Garreth, and though you didn't seem too put out by it, you couldn't have married her, sir. It wouldn't have done, you know."

"Thank you for putting me straight. I might not have known otherwise," Garreth said. "But just how did you manage to save me from what you obviously consider a horrible fate?"

"Well," the young lady said, taking Garreth's hand and inviting him to sit on the confidante facing the chair in which Dorothea sat. Amelia leaned forward, as though prepared to share some marvellous secret with them. Tom and Charlie came to stand behind the small sofa, leaning over, their arms resting on the wood-trimmed back. Lord Glissenton hastily pulled forward two chairs, and while Amelia waited, he and Farrie seated themselves.

"First, I talked Lord Blesser into challenging Lady Ruston to a game of whist," Amelia told them. "She thinks herself a great hand at cards and has wanted to pit her skill against his for ages.''

''Amelia, how did you get him to agree?'' Charlie demanded suspiciously.

''Never mind that,'' Garreth ordered. ''We know Amelia's ways. Get on with the story,'' he urged her.

''So then I found Lady Ruston talking to Mrs. Winstead. I waited until Miss Oglesby was dancing and told her aunt Lord Blesser was waiting, and that Miss Oglesby could join Farrie and Lady Lindsterhope and me between dances until Lady Ruston finished playing cards.''

''And she liked that, since it gave her niece another chance to get her claws into Garreth,'' Charlie said darkly.

''If you want to do all the talking, I'll keep my story to myself,'' Amelia said, frowning at the young marquess.

''You're up in the bows...'' Charlie retorted, but Garreth turned his head to scowl at him.

''Keep quiet, Charlie. Go on, Amelia. We'd best hear the worst of it, since we may have to leave town in the dead of night.''

''When Miss Oglesby came off the floor, I took her aside and told her that her aunt had been taken home, ill, and that we had sent her home in a carriage with Mrs. Furston. I knew Miss Oglesby wouldn't see Mrs. Furston, since she was also in the card room.'' Amelia leaned forward again, her face a vision of triumph. ''And this is the good part. I told her, since the street outside was so full of vehicles that Uncle Garreth was having the horses put to a coach in our stables, and he'd meet her at the back gate and whisk her straight to Ruston House.''

"You were going to send Lord Tolver with her?'' Tom was too caught up in the story to see further than Amelia had told them. "You *knew* how that female had been—''

"Of course she did,'' Dorothea interjected, calming Tom. "Go on, Amelia. I'm interested in how you convinced her.''

"Oh, I knew she'd not let herself in for censure unless she'd a good chance of trapping Uncle Garreth,'' Amelia said. "I told her I had a domino ready, and to be sure no one recognized her, she was to keep her head down so that the hood covered her face and wasn't to speak until they reached Ruston House. After all, there would be stable boys and coachmen in the mews.''

"I hope you'll forgive my outburst of pride,'' Garreth said with a terrible calm, "but how did you get her to accept Palvley in my stead? She certainly couldn't have taken him for me. I'm a good two inches taller than he is.''

"But if she was only looking down, all gentlemen's striped stockings and dancing slippers look alike,'' Dorothea interposed.

"Especially in the dark,'' Farrie added.

"And he didn't get *in* the carriage with her,'' Amelia explained. "And on a horse, the difference in height isn't noticeable.''

"What horse?'' Garreth sounded ominous.

"Greythorne." She clutched Garreth's arm as if he might suddenly spring up and go dashing out of the room in pursuit of his new mount.

"Which would certainly convince Miss Oglesby that you were accompanying her, since everyone knows the animal," Dorothea said soothingly. "And as much as you might value the horse, Garreth, I'm much of the opinion that he is a small price to be rid of both Miss Oglesby and Sir Gerald."

"And Sir Gerald will return him," Amelia said. "He didn't at all like taking him, you know. He may be a rake, but he would not be received in society again if he were thought to be a common horse thief."

"There's nothing common about Greythorne," Garreth snapped.

"But what will happen when she finds he is not taking her to Ruston House?" Farrie asked.

"She'll think she's finally won him over and they're eloping. He'll think it's me in the carriage, and they'll be on their way to Gretna Green before they know the difference."

"Too far to return, since they'll probably travel all night," Charlie said, though he didn't look pleased. "I still say you could have let us in on it."

"But it was a good plan," Tom said, giving Amelia due credit.

After the spate of disclosures they sat silent for a few moments, each considering what had taken place. Then Lord Glissenton spoke up.

"As strange as it may sound, sir, I believe it's the best thing that could have happened. I've no doubt both Miss Oglesby and Sir Gerald would have suc-

ceeded in their plans. Two other people would have
been trapped when they failed with you and Lady
Amelia. Now they both have what they were after,
Miss Oglesby a husband accepted in society, and Sir
Gerald a wife wealthy enough to keep him out of the
sponging houses.''

Garreth's thoughtful frown rested on the young lord
for a moment before he nodded, ''Old Oglesby is a
cit—he'll hold the reins on her money—so Sir Gerald
can't run through it.'' His frown deepened as he stared
at Glissenton. ''How did you get involved in these
cracked-brained schemes?''

''At first I thought I'd stay on the fringes to help
when they found themselves in a mess—''

''I like that!'' Amelia said.

Charlie's hot rejoinder came at the same time. ''We
didn't invite you!''

''And then I found I couldn't resist,'' the young lord
finished with a rueful smile.

Amelia slipped her hand into Garreth's.

''Uncle Garreth, I didn't mean to hurt you, you
know. Sometimes men can't seem to see what's good
for them. She would have been a terrible wife for
you.''

Garreth put both hands on Amelia's shoulders and
gave her a little shake.

''She would have gotten her just deserts. You baggage, she would have had to put up with you always
being underfoot—''

''But I cannot help being about, Uncle Garreth,''
Amelia broke in, her eyes dancing, and not a whit
chastened by his strictures. ''I live here, you see.''

"Wherever you are you'll keep Charlie, Tom, Farrie and probably the rest of us involved in your starts and schemes," Garreth went on, refusing to be put off by her levity. "And that's too much to wish on any woman." He turned from Amelia to Dorothea where she still sat in the chair, feeling drained.

"Sweet Doro, if you want to reconsider your acceptance, I'll understand. You realize we'll have all four of them underfoot until we can marry them off or drown them? We'll be in Bedlam by the end of the year."

"You've made Doro an offer?" Charlie said, astonished.

"I don't b-believe it!" Tom was just as startled. "Good for you, sir, and for us."

"Oh, Doro, I'm so happy for you," Farrie said, rushing to Dorothea.

"Now see!" Amelia turned to Charlie and Tom. "I told you that story of yours wouldn't do any good. Uncle Garreth is too plump in the pocket to care whether Doro has a fortune or not."

"Their story?" Dorothea demanded, jerked out of her wonder. She gazed accusingly at Tom and Charlie. "*You* started that odious rumour?"

"We didn't mean any harm," Tom said as his cheeks reddened. "I m-mean, you seemed flustered when I teased you after Sir Gerald said you might want to marry again, and I thought maybe you did."

"Well, thank you, sprig, but from now on, when we want your help with our affairs we'll let you know," Garreth said. "I can see I'll have to keep a firm hand on the reins. I've never seen such a misbegotten team."

"Oh, not a team, sir," Tom contradicted him. "It will either be five or you'll be driving unicorn." He turned to smile at Farrie who blushed furiously as Lord Glissenton took her hand.

Tom puffed out his chest. "As head of the family I've given Lord Glissenton leave to offer for Farrie." Suddenly he seemed hesitant. "Subject to Doro's approval, and now I suppose yours, sir."

"Farrie." Dorothea embraced her ward and they both shed a few tears while Amelia stood by smiling, and though she didn't by any word claim it, her expression showed she felt a certain justification in sharing the triumph.

"I'm hoping this meets with your approval, sir," Lord Glissenton said to Garreth.

"Well, you won't find that out tonight, because I've had as much of this thundering herd's affairs as I can take. I've matters of my own to see to," he said, clapping the younger man on the back just as the drapery was pulled aside and Lady Jersey entered the room.

"Here you are!" she said as if accusing them of some dark and nefarious deed. "It's really the outside of enough for all of you to disappear at once and remain away so long. Lady Amelia, it is, after all, your ball—" she frowned at Amelia "—her houseguests—" Dorothea and the younger Sailings received a censurous look "—and the best friends of the family." Then it was Charlie's and Garreth's turn. "You realize you are causing talk by your absence?"

Then her disapproving eye fell on the domino and satin slip that had been cast aside and lay forgotten on the floor.

"And what may I ask . . . ?" She cast her frustrated gaze at the ceiling. "I really do not want to know."

"We'll tell you all about it over tea tomorrow, Sally," Garreth said. "In the meantime, be a good sort and cover for us."

"No." She spat out the word. "Garreth, you have coerced me for the last time. Tonight I am going to free myself of the need to cover for your social atrocities. You wait right here!"

"Now what's that all about?" Garreth asked, giving Dorothea a puzzled frown.

"I think we've pushed her too far," she answered softly. "We will be banished to the country before the night is over. Tom, do something about those things."

While Tom gathered up the offending garments, Charlie jerked open the doors of a Chinese lacquered cabinet and they stuffed the clothing inside. Amelia was bemoaning the ruin of her new slip and Farrie was sighing for the crushing of the domino when Lady Jersey returned, carrying a celery-green satin evening cloak over her arm. It appeared to be hanging somewhat stiffy, until she pulled it aside and held out an imperious hand.

In it was a bright, shining, new hoop.

"I refuse to be blackmailed any longer, Garreth. Here is a hoop to make up for the one in the oak tree, and may you have the pleasure of it." Her gaze turned to the spot where the clothing had lain, now empty, and only those that knew her very well would have noticed the slight dimming of her bright eyes, the disappointment of unsatisfied curiosity. She still appeared disapproving, but her voice softened as it took on a hint of entreaty. "I will see the two of you for tea tomorrow." And with that she marched out of the room.

"That's a nice hoop," Amelia said, moving forward to touch the slender circle of steel. "It's larger than the one you had, Charlie."

"You should know, you had the use of it as much as I did," he retorted, though he, too, came forward to feel it. "I wonder if I can still keep it going five paces with one touch of a stick."

"Get your grubby hands off my hoop!" Garreth demanded. "Furthermore, Sally is right, you should get back to the ball and stay out of mischief. We've seen enough of you for a while."

When the five younger members of the group moved off and the argument between Charlie and Amelia over which one had rolled his hoop the fastest had faded in the distance, Garreth made use of his new toy. Pulling Dorothea close to him, he flipped the metal circle down around them both. Though, as he stepped closer and caught her in a tender embrace, he let it go and it fell to the carpet with a soft ring.

"Garreth, are you sure?" Dorothea asked, still doubtful. "The four of them together are worse than two and two, and they'll be up to rigs and romps for years before they settle down. Are you sure you won't get weary of them and me?"

"Weary us, yes, but they won't worry us overmuch." His smile was full of pride. "Our part of the battle is over. They'll mess up a little, but barring big trouble, they can look after themselves."

"After what Tom did—"

"In keeping Tom from going to the moneylenders, Charlie showed what he was made of, and Tom really saved my bacon, you know."

"How?"

"When Miss Oglesby pretended to swoon, I thought he had seen it. Later I thought I had been mistaken, but I wasn't. He had gone for you."

"He did." She was much struck.

"And we'll leave Amelia to John and Harry. They've always said she'd recover from her stumbles." He pulled her closer. "So all we have to think about is us. Let me hear no more about that young horde. We've so much time to make up for, Doro."

"We'll just have to laugh twice as hard, smile twice as often."

"And love twice as much," he said, dropping a gentle kiss on her forehead.

"But as much as I hate to share you with anyone," she said, "I suppose we should be getting back to the ballroom, or we will really be in Sally's black book."

"I'm not worried about Sally. I still have an ace up my sleeve."

"Oh?"

"She still has my ice skates," he grinned with a boyishness that brought back younger, happier days. Dorothea could not resist reaching up to stroke his cheek as she smiled and shook her head.

"No, Garreth, I had your ice skates."

"Oh, Lord, then it's back to the ball, and we'll continue this tomorrow," he murmured, giving her another kiss.

"And tomorrow, and tomorrow, and tomorrow."

"And all the rest of our tomorrows," he said as he led her out of the room.

Harlequin Regency Romance™

COMING NEXT MONTH

#11 VANESSA by Clarice Peters

Vanessa Whitmore, twenty-four, has no claim on beauty, but she is an "original." When her fiancé seemingly jilts her to marry Viscount Peregren's intended, Vanessa and Perry become the talk of the town. Overhearing the Viscount call her an "antidote" is enough to cause a scene, and Vanessa is banished to the country, from whence she is summoned to France. Viscount Peregren, against his better judgment, becomes involved, and soon finds himself amidst fiancés found, fiancés jilted, lovers crossed, duels designated, smuggled bodies and schemes aplenty, until the only solution that will answer is to marry Vanessa and keep her out of trouble!

#12 SOPHIE'S HALLOO by Patricia Wynn

Sophia Corby was declared a changeling by her father. She was his only offspring who didn't care a fig for hunting. Now that she was nineteen, it was time to marry her off. Preferably to someone of his choice. Sophie's gentle nature was immediately attracted to Sir Tony Farnham, for he enjoyed town life immensely and felt no need to hunt. Displeased with his daughter's preference, Sir Corby put forward a Corinthian no one could resist. But the deepening ties between Sophie and Tony could not be torn asunder by her father's will or by a Corinthian's charm, and Tony's patience and generous nature finally ran the fox to the ground.

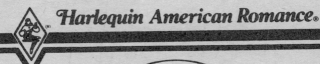

Harlequin American Romance®

Gull Cottage

SUMMER.

The sun, the surf, the sand...

One relaxing month by the sea was all Zoe, Diana and Gracie ever expected from their four-week stays at Gull Cottage, the luxurious East Hampton mansion. They never thought they'd soon be sharing those long summer days—or hot summer nights—with a special man. They never thought that what they found at the beach would change their lives forever. But as Boris, Gull Cottage's resident mynah bird said: "Beware of summer romances...."

Join Zoe, Diana and Gracie for the summer of their lives. Don't miss the GULL COTTAGE trilogy in American Romance: #301 *Charmed Circle* by Robin Francis (July 1989), #305 *Mother Knows Best* by Barbara Bretton (August 1989) and #309 *Saving Grace* by Anne McAllister (September 1989).

GULL COTTAGE—because a month can be the start of forever...

JAYNE ANN KRENTZ WINS HARLEQUIN'S AWARD OF EXCELLENCE

With her October Temptation, *Lady's Choice*, Jayne Ann Krentz marks more than a decade in romance publishing. We thought it was about time she got our *official* seal of approval—the Harlequin Award of Excellence.

Since she began writing for Temptation in 1984, Ms Krentz's novels have been a hallmark of this lively, sexy series—and a benchmark for all writers in the genre. *Lady's Choice*, her eighteenth Temptation, is as stirring as her first, thanks to a tough and sexy hero, and a heroine who is tough when she has to be, tender when she chooses....

The winner of numerous booksellers' awards, Ms Krentz has also consistently ranked as a bestseller with readers, on both romance and mass market lists. *Lady's Choice* will do it for her again!

This lady is *Harlequin's* choice in October.

Available where Harlequin books are sold.

AE-LC-1

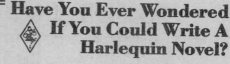

Have You Ever Wondered If You Could Write A Harlequin Novel?

Here's great news—Harlequin is offering a series of cassette tapes to help you do just that. Written by Harlequin editors, these tapes give practical advice on how to make your characters—and your story— come alive. There's a tape for each contemporary romance series Harlequin publishes.

Mail order only

All sales final

TO: ***Harlequin Reader Service***
Audiocassette Tape Offer
P.O. Box 1396
Buffalo, NY   14269-1396

I enclose a check/money order payable to HARLEQUIN READER SERVICE® for $9.70 ($8.95 plus 75¢ postage and handling) for EACH tape ordered for the total sum of $_____ *
Please send:

☐ Romance and Presents   ☐ Intrigue
☐ American Romance   ☐ Temptation
☐ Superromance   ☐ All five tapes ($38.80 total)

Signature_____
Name:_____
                                              (please print clearly)
Address:_____
State:_____ Zip:_____
*Iowa and New York residents add appropriate sales tax.

AUDIO-H

COMING SOON...

Indulge a Little
Give a Lot

An irresistible opportunity to pamper
yourself with free* gifts and help a
great cause, Big Brothers/Big Sisters
Programs and Services.

*With proofs-of-purchase plus postage and handling.

Watch for it in October!

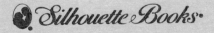